2 8

JOURNEY TO AN ISLAND

JOURNEY TO AN ISLAND

Hilary Wilde

CHIVERS

British Library Cataloguing in Publication Data available

This Large Print edition published by BBC Audiobooks Ltd, Bath, 2009.
Published by arrangement with the Author's Estate.

U.K. Hardcover ISBN 978 1 408 44208 1
U.K. Softcover ISBN 978 1 408 44209 8

Printed and bound in Great Britain by
CPI Antony Rowe, Chippenham and Eastbourne

CHAPTER ONE

'This must surely be the happiest day of your life,' the tall, powerfully-built man said in an odd voice.

Mia looked up and saw the sceptical amusement in his grey eyes. His was not a handsome nor an ugly face, but it was striking. His nose was hawklike, his chin square. His hair was short, thick and dark. But it was his eyes, his grey eyes that never stopped staring at her that were striking. He seemed much bigger and more virile close to, his lean wiry body seemed to throw out a strange magnetism. Mia had the oddest feeling—that suddenly every other person in the room had vanished and they were completely alone.

'It most certainly is,' she replied quickly, her voice stiff.

Mia was nineteen, tall, slender with honey-brown hair. Not pretty, but most people turned to look at her. Perhaps it was her eyes, unexpectedly green. On the third finger of her left hand was her engagement ring, given her that day by Ian Yates, the man she had known and loved all her life. This ball was being given by his parents to introduce her to their friends. Of course she was happy, she thought, suddenly annoyed with this arrogant man.

He had done nothing else but stare at her

1

ever since he walked through the big oaken door into the lofty hall, with its white pillars decorated with golden roses to match the deep yellow carpet, and the chandeliers throwing scintillating light on to the beautiful and colourful clothes of the women guests. He had taken his place in the long queue of guests as they advanced slowly down towards the reception line, there to be greeted by Ian's parents, and introduced to Mia.

Every time she glanced down the line, he was staring at her, a strange, narrowed, searching stare—inscrutable, a little unnerving. She had felt nervous enough before, but he made it a thousand times worse. She fiddled restlessly with the heavy ruby ring that kept sliding down her finger so that she was terrified it might slide off—or fidgeted with her hair, worried lest it collapse and shame her. Once he met her eyes and gave her an amused, rather contemptuous smile, and she had had the strange feeling that it pleased him to know he was making her feel uncomfortable.

Of course she was happy, she thought indignantly. Shouldn't she be? And then, glancing up at the silent man by her side, she admitted to herself the truth.

She was not happy. Everything—but everything, had gone wrong and the little pinpricks of that day had mounted.

The first pinprick had been the ring. Even

as she had exclaimed at the beauty of the ruby, her heart had sunk and she had wished Ian had asked her which was her favourite jewel. Unfortunately she loathed rubies. In addition, it was much too elaborate a style for her liking. And too expensive.

'It's too beautiful . . .' she had begun, and Ian had kissed her.

'Nothing is too good for you,' he had said.

And she had known in her heart the truth: Ian had not chosen the ring, nor had he paid for it. The Yates had chosen the sort of ring they considered suitable for their only son's fiancée.

Her gown had been another pinprick. Mia had already chosen hers, a simple but elegant cream brocade, but Mrs. Yates had said—again most charmingly—that white and cream were for brides, and had insisted on buying the dress Mia was wearing. It was indeed beautiful, the sort of gown film stars wear to make an 'entrance'. Cyclamen-pink silk, it shimmered and shone as she moved. Empress style, it had a very low neckline and a high waist, the silk falling in pleats to the ground. Her father had smiled rather wryly and called it 'eye-shocking', but when she told him she hated it and would refuse to wear it, he had been shocked.

'You can't be so rude, darling. Mrs. Yates is being kind,' he had said.

Mia had managed to smile tolerantly, but

she had known that he was wrong. It had not been kindness on Mrs. Yates' part but fear lest their son's fiancée should disgrace them by wearing a gown that did not scream money.

So Mia had stood there under the bright lights, growing every moment more miserable, more uncertain of her future. Ian was the only man in her life. She had met him as a child and always loved him, but when, six months earlier, he had suddenly asked her to be his wife, and she had said yes without having to pause and think, she had never realised what marrying a Yates would mean. It had begun when Ian joined the family firm of stockbrokers and started to be groomed as a young executive. Mia knew that now she, too, was being groomed—to be a young executive's wife! Ian had changed so much, become more ambitious, earnest, always talking about the importance of 'friends'. Only that day he had told her that a very important man was coming to the ball.

'Gideon Eastwood.' He had said the name reverently. 'He's a millionaire. He inherited half his fortune and the other half he made himself. Brilliant, he has terrific contacts. Now if only I could land him as a client, my father would be so pleased . . . So, darling, be especially nice to him,' Ian had begged.

Glancing at Ian's mother, statuesquely tall and dignified, tightly-corseted and perfectly made-up, in a gown that matched the roses on the pillars, Mia wondered if she could ever be like Mrs. Yates. Or, what had suddenly become even more important, if she wanted to be like her.

Ian's father was stockily-built, with snow-white hair and a bland smile. He and his wife were perfectionists, and that night, for the first time, Mia had wondered if she could ever satisfy them.

It had been as she was thinking this that Ian had nudged her gently, whispering significantly: 'This is the man . . .' and she had looked up into the cold grey searching eyes of the man who had stared at her.

'I'd like you to meet my fiancée, Mr. Eastwood,' Ian began, then went bright red. 'Mia, I mean, I'd like to introduce . . .' his voice had petered out unhappily as Gideon Eastwood took charge.

'I wish you every happiness, Miss Barton, and I congratulate you on your good fortune, Yates,' the tall, arrogant-looking man said smoothly, his voice deep, his words slightly pedantic, Mia thought.

She was startled to realise suddenly that she disliked him. Was it because of his voice that sounded as if he was accustomed to shouting orders and having people leap to obey them?

'This must surely be the happiest day of your life,' he had added, and she had known then that he was mocking her.

But why? Why?

5

Ian was talking fast, too fast, about nothing. Looking at them both, Mia was struck by the complete difference in the two men. True, Ian was only twenty-four whereas Gideon Eastwood must be in his mid-thirties, but Ian looked even younger with his round cheeks, cerulean-blue eyes and that sweet shy smile, whereas Gideon Eastwood had an air of self-confidence, a look of success.

'When do you plan to marry?' he asked.

Mia lifted her pointed chin. It was a little habit of defiance she was not aware of.

'In six months,' she said coolly.

Gideon Eastwood went on staring at her and she fidgeted, feeling her new shoes pinching her toes.

'I beg your pardon,' he said unexpectedly. 'Was I staring?'

'You have been ever since you arrived,' Mia said coldly, and heard Ian's little gasp of dismay. She realised she had sounded rude, so she smiled. 'I was afraid my hair was falling down,' she added lightly.

She could feel Ian relax by her side as Gideon Eastwood laughed. 'On the contrary, it looks well-disciplined. I apologise for my rudeness, Miss Barton. The trouble is I seem to know your face. You know how it is when you meet someone with a face you recognise yet you can't pinpoint who the other person was . . .'

Ian laughed, a little too loudly, Mia thought.

She turned to smile at him reassuringly and thought how young he looked and unsure, so very different from this arrogant man who was precariously balanced on the edge of being pompous, she thought. She knew that in a crowd, all eyes would be turned on Gideon Eastwood. Not only for his size, or for his handsome elegance in his dinner jacket, tailored trousers, and red cummerbund, but because of his air of assurance. Was it his money that gave him that, she wondered, or his success? Ian had said he had many interests, his biggest being that of ship-building.

'May I dance with your fiancée?' Gideon Eastwood asked, glancing at the few guests there were left to be spoken to.

Ian beamed, 'Of course. She's a wonderful dancer, Mr. Eastwood.'

Mia frowned slightly. Surely Gideon Eastwood should have asked her first, she thought. After all, for all he knew, she might hate the very idea of dancing with him. Then she saw Ian's anxious eyes and so she smiled at the tall man and led him through the lavishly-decorated hall to the ballroom.

'This is quite a house, isn't it?' he asked, his hand under her elbow lightly.

'Yes, it is,' she said stiffly. She agreed with his unspoken comment that it was a ghastly house, but she also owed loyalty to Ian. 'The sort of house the glossy magazines love.'

Gideon laughed. 'Yes, and the elegantly-clad hostess is photographed, in a terrifically expensive dress, arranging the flowers that have already been done by a florist.'

Mia found herself laughing, for it was a perfect description. 'It's designed for what is called gracious entertaining,' she said, quick to jump to Ian's parents' defence. But definitely not the kind of house you could live in, she thought. And certainly not the sort of house she and Ian would have.

Gideon stood still and looked at her. There was an oddly derisive smile on his face as if he knew she did not want to dance with him.

'Shall we . . . ?' he asked.

As she moved into his arms, Mia shivered. It was only a momentary, quick reaction, but it startled her. She only reached his shoulder and she kept her head bent so that he could not see her face. It disturbed her, that small electric shock. She had never experienced such a feeling before.

She was surprised how good a dancer he was. Infinitely better than Ian, who was often clumsy in his movements. Gideon Eastwood danced as if he enjoyed every moment of it—just as she did.

She racked her brains trying to think of something to say. She wondered why she felt like this. Her father, although a country vicar, had many distinguished friends and Mia was used to meeting them and talking easily. But tonight there seemed to be an anchor on her tongue or a fog round her brain. She could not think of a single opening remark. What do you talk to a millionaire about? she wondered. His money? His yachts—cars—possessions? Do you talk of the weather or politics? If only she could think of one intelligent thing to say . . . It meant so much to Ian.

'You live near here?' Gideon Eastwood asked casually.

She looked up at him. 'About three miles away. My father is vicar of Hawbridge. That's a small village, one of the few we've left near London.'

'You don't look like a country girl.'

'But I am,' she said quickly, her cheeks slightly red. 'I love village life—hearing the local news, meeting people who've known me all my life.'

He smiled. 'How very different from my life. My real home, if you can call it that, is on an island in the Indian Ocean. I go there whenever I can, but most of my life is divided between London, New York, Paris and Berlin. I get around . . .' He gave a strange, lop-sided grin which seemed to soften his hard face. 'At heart,' he went on, 'I'm a sailor. My family have always built ships and I'm the same. If I could, I'd live at sea.'

She studied his face thoughtfully. It was bronze with suntan, yet he lived in cities. She wondered how he kept looking so full of life

9

and virility.

'But surely,' she said without thinking, 'you can do what you like? I mean, I believe you're very rich . . .'

He gave a rueful smile. 'I have responsibilities.'

The music stopped and he walked back with her to the hall, but Ian had vanished. Gideon Eastwood hesitated, gazing intently at the face lifted politely towards him.

'Where did you meet Ian Yates?' he asked abruptly.

If Mia was startled, she managed to hide it. 'The Yates used to live in Hawbridge before they built this house. I've known Ian all my life.'

'I see . . .' he said thoughtfully, and went on staring at her.

She wondered how she could get rid of him, tactfully and without offence. She wished he would stop staring at her in that way. It made her feel uneasy.

It was as if he read her thoughts. 'Please forgive me,' he said. 'I'm staring again, aren't I? I suppose I should do my duty and ask a few ladies to dance. May I have another dance later?'

She danced most of the evening, passing from one pair of masculine arms to another. She laughed and talked, and occasionally Ian would smile at her as he danced by and she knew his parents were pleased with her.

But the whole time Gideon Eastwood seemed to dominate everything. It began to annoy Mia so much that she felt if she heard his name again she would scream. No one could be as perfect as Gideon Eastwood appeared to be!

Everyone asked her what she thought of him. Deftly she avoided a direct answer, saying he danced well, seemed an interesting man. Everyone talked of Gideon Eastwood's wealth, of his international fame, for apparently he excelled at everything: flying, skiing, deep-sea diving, cricket, rugby, tennis . . . his ability was never-ending.

Dancing briefly with Ian, Mia voiced her feeling. 'He's too perfect to be true,' she said crossly. 'Isn't there something he can't do?'

Ian looked shocked. 'Don't you like him? He told Father I was lucky to win such a beautiful, intelligent girl.'

Mia caught her breath. Of all the sarcastic . . .! She bit back angry words. It was fortunate that Ian's father had not recognised Gideon Eastwood's sarcasm, she thought.

'Everything seems to be going well,' she said, to change the subject.

Ian beamed and tightened his arm round her. 'It is. You're doing wonders, darling. I'm so proud of you. So are the parents. I can always tell when my father's pleased.'

Mia stifled a sigh. It was a good party, she supposed, if you liked this kind of party. She

11

didn't. Yet Ian had told her over and over again that they would have to entertain like this if he was to make any good contacts.

'The personal touch,' he had said, sounding eerily like his father, 'is so very important.'

As the music stopped, Gideon Eastwood came to their side.

'May I?' he said to Ian, and took Mia into his arms. They had danced once round the room when he said, 'I've been talking to your father. He's a wonderful man.'

Mia looked up, her face changing, becoming almost luminous with happiness for a moment, her eyes shining.

'He is,' she agreed warmly.

They danced in silence and then Gideon glanced down.

'I'm feeling hungry. How about something to eat?' he asked. 'Can we find somewhere to sit?' he asked. They went to the buffet table and helped themselves, finding two chairs in a small alcove, under the wide staircase. They were not alone and yet shut off from other people, and Gideon said it would do.

'I'm not a dancing man, though I enjoy it very much when I do,' he said, and turned to stare at her. 'Is Ian?'

Mia hesitated. 'Not really. He does it because—'

'His mother tells him to?' Gideon asked.

It was like a splash of ice-cold water on her. She was so shocked she could not speak. 'I . . .'

12

She stared at Gideon.

He moved his hand impatiently. 'Don't look so horrified—all I mean is, it's a social thing with him, isn't it? his duty etcetera? Now, you—you loving dancing, don't you?'

Mia nodded. 'Yes. Once I dreamed of being a dancer,' she told him, surprised at herself, for few people knew. 'I . . . I was good at ballet and . . .'

He took the empty plate from her hand and put it down on a nearby table. 'Then why aren't you a dancer?' he asked with a smile.

She saw that he had not forgotten that she had asked him why he wasn't a sailor! 'I, too, have responsibilities,' she said.

'*Touché*,' he said, putting back his head to laugh.

Glancing at the groups of people standing and talking, Mia saw Ian's mother glancing at her, nodding her head gently in approval.

'You see,' Mia went on, 'my mother died when I was thirteen. Dad was heartbroken and I knew I could never leave him. I've done my best, but I don't think a daughter can ever be the same as a wife.'

Gideon looked at her. 'I wouldn't know, never having married.'

How had such a man managed to stay single? Mia wondered. She judged him to be in his early thirties.

'Tell me, how did you come to get mixed up with this crowd?' he asked, waving his hand towards the other guests.

Startled by the contempt in his voice, she said, 'You don't like this kind of party?'

'Good grief, of course not. And neither do you, that's—'

'Why come, then?' she asked, irritated by his voice.

He smiled. 'A good question deserves the truth. Because of Ian. I've met him several times and I like him—but I wanted to see what sort of girl was fool enough to marry him.'

Again, Mia caught her breath with the shock of the unexpected attack. It took her a moment to get her voice back.

'Because I love him.'

Gideon Eastwood leant back in his chair, stretching out his long legs, folding his arms. 'Oh no, you don't.'

'I do,' Mia said quickly, and saw the mocking smile on Gideon's face. 'I do love him,' she repeated, but this time her voice was unsteady.

The mocking smile vanished. Gideon looked at her gravely. 'You did love him,' he corrected gently. 'When did you stop loving him?'

She looked round wildly, hoping Ian would see her and rescue her. Then she knew he wouldn't—Gideon Eastwood was too important a person to risk annoying. This was something she must handle alone.

'You've no right to cross-examine me,' she

said, controlling her voice carefully.

Gideon did not look surprised. 'I know—it's a horrible habit I have, so please bear with me.' A quick smile lit up his grave face. 'You're not in court, you know. Nothing you say will be used against you.' He smiled again: 'I just thought it might help you if you talked about it to someone.'

She stared at him, startled by his instinct. How often had she longed during the recent weeks to talk to her father about Ian—but her father had taught her to think for herself. He refused ever to advise her. He might show her two sides to the question, but then the final solution must be hers.

'It's difficult to . . .' Mia began, twisting her fingers and staring at them, avoiding Gideon's cool grey eyes. She thought aloud, bewitched by his silence, finding amazing relief in just talking about it, as he had said she would.

'I've known him since I was a child. He was always kind and patient with me, though I was much younger. Later, we played tennis together, went for picnics. He was rather shy and had few girl-friends. I guess he felt like I did, happy when we were together . . .' She smiled for a moment, glancing quickly at the man by her side. He nodded silently.

'Then—then—' Mia went on, 'about six months ago, after he'd left university and had gone abroad for a holiday, he joined his father's firm and . . .'

'He changed?'

'Yes, completely. Became much more formal. For instance, he always calls his parents Mother and Father now, whereas before it was Mum and Dad. Then—then he always called me Green-eyes, but now it's always Mia. He's worried about his appearance and is always afraid he'll say the wrong thing . . .'

'In other words, he has become the typical ambitious young executive,' Gideon Eastwood said quietly.

Mia looked at him. 'Is it just a phase? Will he grow out of it?'

'Perhaps,' Gideon's smile was rueful. 'Or he may grow exactly like his father.'

Both sat in silence, looking across the hall to where the Yates stood, saying goodbye to some guests. Mia shivered a little as she watched their polite, gracious smiles, the look of boredom on their faces as they turned away and spoke to one another.

'Some women don't mind,' Gideon went on, his voice still quiet. 'His wife loves him. But you don't love Ian enough.'

She turned to him at once, her green eyes dismayed. 'I'll learn . . .'

'Wait,' Gideon said, his hand tightly closing over hers, 'let me finish. Face facts, however unpalatable they are. Ian is a good lad, but with one great weakness, or maybe with two. He is a mother's boy . . .'

Mia's hand flew to her mouth. 'He is not
. . .' she began, the words dying a natural
death, leaving a bitter taste in her mouth, for
they were true.

'He is also terrified of his father,' Gideon
went on. 'I'm not blaming him. We're all made
differently, but the type Ian is can never be
successful. He's too dependent on the advice
of others. He'll never take the initiative or be
able to lead. I'm sorry, for I like him . . .'

Bitter, sarcastic, angry words boiled up
inside Mia. What right, she asked herself, has
he to judge Ian? She fought the anger, for she
must behave with dignity. Let him finish what
he had to say, then she would find an excuse
and leave him. She must not quarrel with
Gideon Eastwood, it meant too much to
Ian . . .

She closed her eyes. The name stabbed her
viciously—Ian, Ian. She was always worrying
about Ian these days. She had loved him and
love didn't die overnight—it was just that he
was tense in his new life, suffering from the
necessary adjustments of the discipline of
office work. Ian would get over it, gain self-
confidence and . . .

'I think I was lucky,' Gideon Eastwood went
on. Mia tried not to listen but, short of sticking
her fingers in her ears which would only upset
Ian and his parents, there was little she could
do. She sat very still, trying to control the
anger building up inside her.

17

'My parents died when I was a child. My grandparents brought me up. The old man was a martinet for discipline, he taught me to toe the line, to make decisions and abide by my mistakes. My grandmother taught me not to run to her if I was hurt but to stand alone. It was tough, but I'm grateful. I can walk alone. Ian will never he able to do so, poor devil, he so badly needs encouragement, someone constantly boosting his morale, praising him. Are you prepared to do that for the rest of your life?' He turned and looked at her sharply.

She looked back at him, her face stiff with the effort to control herself. She felt frozen, for Gideon's words had seared their way right into her heart. No matter how much she hated admitting it, she knew he was right.

Looking back, she remembered so much— Ian's dependence on his mother, his anxiety if things went wrong and his father might hear. He was even worse today. It was as if he trod a narrow plank from which he was terrified he might fall. Was that why he had asked her to be his wife? So that she could help him when his mother was not there?

Mia shivered as Gideon took hold of her hands and held them. He had moved his chair so that his back was towards the hall and she was slightly sheltered from any curious gaze. Most of the guests had gone into the other rooms so there was no audience. He leaned forward, his voice grave.

'You're a lovely girl on the threshold of life. Like your father, you're warm-hearted and intelligent. You'll never survive this sort of phoney life.' He jerked his head backwards towards the big hall. 'Pretending to like people because they could be useful to you,' he went on, his voice scornful. 'Acting! I've watched you this evening. You've nearly broken your heart, trying to do something you knew was false. You acted a lie when you tried to be charming and look happy. How can Ian find the security he needs if his wife is unable to help him? How will you manage to live up to the standards the Yates will expect—standards of what, to you, mean degradation? Selling your charm and goodwill, smarming over people you dislike. You'll never do it . . .' He almost spat the words out as unexpectedly he lost his temper: 'And you know it!' he said angrily, standing up, scraping his chair noisily. He pulled Mia to her feet, holding one hand tightly, dropping the other.

'Mia . . .' he said, and everything seemed to stand still; the distant laughter and voices were wiped out.

Mia held her breath. It was a strange moment and they seemed to be alone in the world. His face was strangely taut, his eyes grave as he went on. 'Don't do it,' he said.

For a moment she thought he was pleading with her, but then she knew how wrong she was as she heard the imperious, demanding, arrogant note return to his voice. 'You don't need to marry Ian Yates,' he said. 'There are plenty of rich men in the world if it's money you want.'

Mia acted without thought. The reflex action was almost automatic, the culmination of her growing anger. Her hand moved and she smacked his face . . . even as her hand flew back to her mouth in dismay, her eyes wide, his fingers touched his cheek where she could see the red marks of her fingers.

'I'm—I'm sorry,' she gasped, icy cold with shock. What would Ian say—and his parents? She could hardly breathe, it was as if a hand clutched her throat, throttling her.

Gideon Eastwood looked at her.

'You are not sorry,' he said, 'so don't add insult to injury by pretending that you are. I apologise for what I said. Even if I thought it, I had no right to say such a thing.'

He half-turned, saw that the hall was empty, then looked back at her. She hated his smile as he said: 'Fortunately, you had no audience.'

He began to walk away, stopped dead and turned. 'Incidentally,' he said dryly, 'don't panic. I promise not to tell Mother's Boy what you did.'

He left her standing there, trembling. Trembling as much with anger as with dismay at what she had done.

CHAPTER TWO

Mia bathed her hot cheeks in cold water in the bathroom on the first floor. She had taken a few moments to recover from the shock of slapping Gideon Eastwood's face and hearing his scathing words, and then she had darted up the wide, graceful staircase and along the carpeted corridor until she reached the sanctuary of the bathroom. There she had stood for what seemed an endless time, her hands pressed against her mouth, as she stared miserably at her own reflection.

How could she have done such a terrible thing? she asked herself. Never before—or at least not that she could remember—had she known such instant anger or reacted so quickly to the fury that had filled her.

How dared he say such things to her? Did he think, she wondered, that his millions of pounds entitled him to be as rude as he liked? Yet shouldn't she have acted with dignity and controlled herself, answering him with an icy politeness that could have been more damning than the blow she had given him?

Carefully, methodically, she washed and made up her face, for she was worried in case her anger still showed. Her eyes were too bright, her cheeks flushed, her hands still trembled as she tried to apply lipstick to her unhappy mouth. Gideon Eastwood had said he would tell no one—but could she believe that? she wondered. Or someone might have seen what had happened, discreetly vanished, but be only too glad to tell the story later.

It took courage, but she knew she had no choice, so she went downstairs, merging into the crowd of guests, dancing, laughing and talking. No one seemed to have missed her, nor did anyone comment on her appearance, so she imagined she must look all right.

One bad moment came when, after dancing with Ian's father, the music stopped and, standing still to clap, Mia found that Gideon Eastwood, dancing with Mrs. Yates, was standing by their side, looking at them.

Instinctively Mia caught her breath as she met Gideon's amused and somewhat mocking eyes, and when Mr. Yates said, with an air of gallantry, 'May I dance with my wife, Eastwood? First chance I've had this evening,' Mia wanted to turn and run.

However, there was nothing she could do about it, so she gave her best smile at the plump man who was to he her father-in-law, and turned to Gideon, her face stiff with the effort to smile.

They danced in silence, Mia keeping her eyes downcast, feeling the impersonal way with which he held her, wondering if she should apologise again for losing her temper or if it would only make matters worse. In the end, she could think of nothing to say, so she said nothing. When the dance finished, Gideon walked with her to Ian, who was watching them, his round, plump, youngish face bright with pleasure.

'You're a very lucky man, Yates,' Gideon said curtly, and handed Mia over as if, she thought, she was a parcel to be delivered. 'Thank you, Miss Barton,' Gideon continued, his voice formal, gave a little bow, and left them.

Ian drew Mia into a quiet dark corner at the end of the hall. Taking her in his arms, he kissed her. She turned her head instinctively so that his mouth found her cheek and not her lips.

'Are you angry about something?' he asked, and she heard the anxiety in his voice.

She kissed him, very lightly, and tried to laugh. 'Of course not, just rather tired. So's Dad. I can see—' She looked down the hall to where her father was talking to Mr. and Mrs. Yates. 'I think we should go, Ian, if you don't mind.'

'Of course I mind,' he said with a laugh, then he ran his hand through his light hair. 'I always mind when you go, Mia. I feel—I feel so alone.'

In the half-light, she studied his face carefully.

'I can't always be around,' she said gently. But something inside her seemed to jerk.

23

Wasn't this just what Gideon had said? That Ian needed someone to support him.

Ian smiled. 'You will be—one day,' he told her. 'I can't wait for the day. Darling, the parents think you were wonderful. Gideon Eastwood told them you'll make me a perfect wife . . .'

Mia was glad of the dim light so that she could hide her feelings as swift anger flooded her again. How dared Gideon Eastwood be so sarcastic at her expense? And what right had he to judge and condemn Ian? She wondered what Ian and his parents would think if they knew Gideon's real opinion of Ian.

'I must go . . .' she said worriedly.

Her father looked relieved when she joined him. The Yates were friendly but did not press them to stay longer, but Mia saw that both were pleased with her. It made her feel worse, ashamed of the truth, tempted to tell them what she thought of their wonderful Gideon Eastwood.

It was cold outside and she shivered despite the fur-lined coat she wore over her evening dress. Her father, by her side, started the quietly expensive black car. She thought he looked tired and even a little worried. His strong face with the thick white hair looked different in the moonlight, she thought. For the first time, he looked old. She wondered what had happened to upset him.

'It was quite a party, Daddy,' she said. 'I felt

24

a bit overwhelmed.'

He smiled as he looked at her. 'So did I, Mia. But the Yates are rather overwhelming, aren't they? I mean, it's part of their uniform, isn't it? Overwhelmingly rich, overwhelmingly successful, overwhelmingly charming. You'll get used to it in time.'

'Will I?' she said wistfully. 'I wonder if I'll get like that—overwhelmingly awful.'

He laughed. 'I doubt it.'

'Sometimes I wonder if I really want to . . .'

'Don't worry, Mia,' he said gently, 'this is only your engagement, your testing time. What the dictionary describes as a "means of trial". This is the time during which you and Ian can discover if you love one another enough for the trials of matrimony. Marriage isn't all honey, Mia. You'll be expected to adjust and adapt yourself, to conform to things you dislike. If you love Ian enough, you'll do it. If not . . .' He paused as he deftly negotiated a U-turn that led to their village, 'then you can break off the engagement. Far better to do that than go on with a marriage you're not sure about.'

His words were, as always, impersonal. He would never try to influence her.

Not as Gideon Eastwood had done, Mia thought, shivering despite the warm coat. Yet his words had been very similar to her father's. Gideon had said she did not love Ian enough.

Yet what right, she thought angrily, had

25

Gideon to judge the depths of her love for Ian? And why was she letting him influence her? She had only talked to Gideon Eastwood for—for half an hour? An hour at most, but already he had undermined her love for Ian. Yet—that small inner voice asked her—if she was sure about her love for Ian, could the words of a cruelly arrogant man, obviously spoiled by his great wealth, have the power to come between them?

'What did you think of Gideon Eastwood?' her father asked abruptly.

Unprepared for the question, Mia told the truth: 'I hate him!'

Her father looked at her. 'I liked him,' he said mildly.

She slid along the seat to be near him, burrowing her face in his arm as she had so often done as a child. 'You like everyone, Daddy,' she said with affectionate indulgence. 'Maybe I'm just tired.'

'Yes, darling, it was a trying time for you. Like being a butterfly pinned to a specimen board . . .'

'Or a goldfish swimming in a bowl,' Mia added, grateful for his understanding.

'You'll get used to it,' he told her comfortingly. 'You did well, darling. I was proud of you.'

Confession trembled on her tongue as she longed to tell the truth. What would he say if he knew that she had lost her temper with

26

Gideon Eastwood and slapped his face? What would her father's opinion of her be? He had brought her up to control herself. Yet . . .

She drew a long deep breath. Suddenly she knew why she had been so angry. She also knew that Gideon Eastwood's insult had only been the last straw that had triggered off her impulsive action. It had really been because—before that last accusing lie—he had told her the truth; that Ian was weak and dominated by his parents, that she should be ashamed of herself for being charming to people, including himself, simply in order to help Ian and his father make money out of them. That was the real reason for her anger, the fact that she had not liked being told the truth!

She had not expected to sleep well that night, but she fell into a comfortable blackness as she shut her eyes and did not waken until her early morning cup of tea arrived.

She was icing a cake for one of the children she taught when Ian arrived. Mia was startled to see him, for he had told her he was taking his mother out to lunch.

'Mia darling, I must tell you something,' he said excitedly. 'Get your coat. I've got a half-hour to spare and we'll go to the primrose dell. I simply must tell you . . .'

He looked so happy she had not the heart to tell him that she was too busy, that she had the cake to ice, the shopping to do, and was lunching with some friends.

'I'll get my coat,' she said.

Five minutes later, in his red sports car, they were driving out of the village to their favourite picnic spot. Few people knew of it. Just a group of wand-like trees on the side of the hill where the first primroses always appeared.

He parked the car and for a moment both sat in silence, looking at the valley below that stretched away into the hazy distance. The sky was blue, the sun unexpectedly warm. The Thames was a silvery ribbon winding its way through neatly-hedged fields, half-hidden by the trees that leaned over the cool water.

'Just wait,' Ian said, his voice unsteady. She saw that his hands were shaking with excitement as he undid a briefcase. 'Now remember, Mia,' he said with a strange solemnity, 'this must be a secret between us. If the parents knew I was telling you, they'd be furious. But I knew how thrilled you'd be, so I simply had to tell you . . .'

He was spreading papers before them. Puzzled by his excitement, Mia stared at them and suddenly felt her body stiffen. She was gazing at the architect's plan of a house. By the side was a drawing of the house as it would look when finished. An impressive house, was her first thought. A terrifying building, her second. Automatically her eyes followed Ian's finger as he talked, pointing to the different items.

'See, Mia, these pillars support the wide balcony. It gives us a terrace for entertaining on when it's hot. This is designed for us to entertain . . . these rooms lead out of one another. On the first floor will be our cosy rooms, as the architect calls them—our bedrooms. My study, your workroom, whatever you like to call it, and a sitting-room. Then here we'll have the—the . . .' He turned to smile at her. 'The nursery. There's a flat for the nanny. And top floor is for the staff . . .'

'Ian, we can't afford a house like this,' Mia said.

His face was radiant. 'The parents are giving it to us, Mia. They want to surprise you, though, that's why it's a secret. We'll have a swimming pool, garage for three cars, tennis court . . . It's going to be terrific!'

Mia could hardly speak. 'Where will we live?'

'They're looking for the right place now, Mia. Not too far from London yet in the country.'

'But—but I thought we were getting married in six months? It could never be ready . . .'

Ian laughed excitedly. 'Of course it will. Money talks, Mia, and. . . and most wonderful of all, darling, Dad's treating us to a world tour for our honeymoon. Aren't they generous?'

Mia found it hard to smile. 'They are!'

It was as if something had died inside her.

How could she accept this? A house she disliked at first sight, for it was too brash and ambitious for them in their youth. She had planned a small house which they would hurry back to from their honeymoon—she had even worked out her routine for the days, the good meal waiting for Ian when he came home, tired. It had been a lovely thought . . . just the two of them. She tried to smile and wanted to cry. Had she been so blind and stupid, she wondered, as not to realise that the Yates would completely dominate their lives?

'Isn't it a beautiful house, Mia?' Ian went on eagerly, as if not noticing her silence. 'Ideal for the entertaining we'll have to do. Mother says you wear your clothes so elegantly that there's no reason why, one day, you shouldn't be one of the best dressed women in the world,' he finished proudly.

Mia opened her mouth, but the words would not come. Ian was so happy—so thrilled by it all. How could she tell him the truth— that she could not face the sort of life he planned, a life in which she, as well as Ian, would be a puppet, dangling on the string the Yates jerked.

Ian glanced at his watch, his face suddenly worried. 'Gosh! I'd no idea we were so long. I told Mum I'd just pop down and tell you how beautiful you looked last night.'

She knew how happy he was because he was calling his parents Mum and Dad again and

30

now, as he turned and gave her a smile of singular sweetness, she wanted to cry. How could she hurt him? Why hadn't she realised earlier what marriage to one of the Yates would mean?

He drove her back fast, but slowed up as they reached the village square with the Cross in the centre of the road.

'What's up?' Ian asked. 'Looks like an accident . . .'

Mia's heart seemed to jerk. Not knowing why, she was suddenly frightened as she saw Mrs. Hartley standing, openly weeping, and Mrs. White in the doorway of the Post Office, her hands pressed to her mouth, while George Saul, the butcher, was shouting angrily at the policeman who was making notes.

Ian drew the car up and Mike Johnson put away his notebook and came to their side. He ran his finger round inside his collar, his face flushed and unhappy.

'It's bad news, Mia,' he said gently. He had known her since she was a child, and loved him tossing her in the air with his big gentle hands. 'It's your dad. Knocked down by . . .'

'A hit-and-run driver,' George Saul said angrily, joining them. 'Your dad was walking home from the church. I saw it happen and rushed out, but the car was gone like a streak of lightning and I only got the last two numbers, but—'

'That wasn't much help,' Mike Johnson said

31

quietly. 'Pipe down, there's a good fellow, this is bad enough for Mia . . .' He put his hands on the side of the red car and looked gravely at Mia. 'The ambulance came and took him. It might be an idea if you went to the hospital right away.'

Mia's mouth was dry, her face stiff with fear. She knew what Mike Johnson was trying to tell her, though he did not want to put it into words.

'I'll go now,' she said. She glanced at Ian. 'You'll take me.' It was a statement and not a question, and she wondered at his momentary hesitation.

'Of course,' he said.

The market town was crowded and Mia tried to be patient, knowing that Ian could not do more, but when they went up the hill towards the big new hospital that overlooked and dominated the town, she relaxed with relief. It wouldn't be so bad once she was there with him, if she could hold his hand tightly and pray . . . It was not knowing—fearing . . .

Glancing at Ian, she wondered at his white face, his air of tension. And then she remembered how he feared illness and even the sight of blood; remembering how once when she had fallen from her horse and cut her leg to the bone, he had quietly fainted.

'Just drop me, Ian,' Mia said gently. 'Your mother's expecting you. Ring me at the hospital later.'

There was something pathetic about the relief on his face, that was followed by an uneasy shame as he stared at her. 'Will you be all right?'

'Of course,' she said, feeling the sharp pain as her nails cut her skin. 'I know everyone here, the doctors and Matron. I'll be quite all right.'

He walked up the wide steps of the hospital with her. 'I do hope he'll be okay,' he said awkwardly. 'If there's anything I can do . . .'

Yes, there is, she wanted to scream, hold me tight, tell me that it's all a nightmare, that Daddy is at home, grumbling, with laughter in his eyes, because I'm late for lunch. Tell me everything is all right. Just hold me very tightly so that it hurts . . .

Instead she smiled: 'I know, Ian. Don't worry, I'm sure Dad will be all right.'

Quickly she plunged into the lofty coolness of the hall, hating the usual smell of disinfectant, the sight of white-clad nurses and orderlies wheeling trolleys or stretchers. She went straight to the desk.

'Room fifteen, Miss Barton—but ask the Sister before you go in,' the thin, grey-headed woman said gently. 'They may be operating or preparing him.'

Mia went up in the lift, a modern lift whose doors closed with ominous gentleness, enclosing her in what looked like a box, giving no sign of movement, so that she wanted to

33

scream, to beat on the doors—but before she could, the doors politely slid open and she could walk out.

Dr. Lombard, thin, austere-looking, with the eyes of a man who refuses to be defeated, came to her, taking both her hands in his.

'You can't see him yet,' he said gently. 'We may have to operate—we're not sure. Go and sit down and pray. We'll need all the help we can get.'

Obediently she sat in the small, cold waiting-room, staring blindly at the vase of artificial poppies that looked horribly like blood. She closed her eyes to shut them out, and her mind searched round for the right prayer. She chose the twenty-third Psalm: 'The Lord is my shepherd . . .'

She must have said it a thousand times, she thought, before she heard a footstep and opened her eyes again. But it was Matron with a strong, sweet cup of tea.

'What's wrong? What happened to him?' Mia demanded, the questions she had not dared to ask before, now tumbling out.

Matron sat down. 'A couple of broken ribs, a broken arm, injury to one leg and—' she hesitated—'we're not sure yet about internal injuries. He lost a lot of blood, but—' she smiled—'try not to worry, Miss Barton. Your father is tough.'

'Why has it to be Daddy?' Mia cried. 'He's so good . . .'

Matron comforted her. 'I know,' she said again, 'it's a question we always ask. But try to be brave. There's every chance he'll be all right.'

It seemed lonelier than ever when Matron left and Mia began to pace up and down, feeling she was in prison. Supposing her father was injured internally, supposing he was an invalid for the rest of his life? How he would hate it.

She stood at the window and watched the bustle and traffic in the market below. Never had she felt so alone.

She found herself thinking of Gideon Eastwood. He wouldn't have left her, she knew that.

The door opened and Dr. Lombard came in, wearing white trousers and jacket, his small white cap perched on top of his bald head and the mask dangling under his chin. For a moment he looked so comic she wanted to giggle, but she stifled it, knowing she was horribly near hysteria.

'You can see your father now, Miss Barton. He's conscious and in no pain. He has something he must tell you. It troubles him greatly. I don't feel it's wise to let him talk for long, but if, on the other hand, I refuse to let him, I think the effect on him would be disastrous.'

'Something to tell me?' Mia echoed, puzzled.

Dr. Lombard nodded. 'Something he considers very grave. It's troubling his conscience.'

'But I can't imagine anything—'

The doctor smiled. 'I agree, neither can I, but it's worrying him very much, and I don't think we'll progress until he gets this off his mind.'

They walked down the corridor together, Mia looking ahead, studiously avoiding glancing through the glass doors, to the small private ward. What could her father have to tell her that was so urgent? she wondered.

Dr. Lombard put his hand on her hand. 'One word of warning, child. Don't be shocked when you see him. It looks worse than it is.'

Mia nodded, but as the door opened and they went inside, she caught her breath with horror. Surely nothing could look or seem worse? Her father was swathed in bandages, on each side were jars of liquid being fed into the veins of his arms. He was white and drawn, but he turned his head and smiled.

'I'm in no pain, child,' he said gently.

Mia sat down and took his hand in hers. His hand was limp and damp, but his fingers tightened round hers.

'I have so much to tell you, Mia,' he said very slowly. 'I should have told you years ago, for now I'm afraid I may hurt you . . .'

She slid to her knees by the side of the bed and put her hand against his cheek, trying to

36

send some of the warmth of her body into him, to give him some of her strength.

'Nothing you could ever say would hurt me, Daddy darling,' she promised.

Behind her, she heard the door close gently, and then her father began to talk.

*   *   *

It was dark when she left the hospital. They had been very kind to her, Matron wanting to send someone home with her, but Mia had lied in desperation, saying Ian was waiting for her. It was also cold, and Mia moved stiffly down the steps to the street. She did not feel alive. It was as if some other power than her own forced her limbs to move.

Her whole world had been turned upside down—her security destroyed. She no longer knew anything about herself. She felt like a tiny ant, alone, afraid, unloved, scurrying wildly to escape from a horror she had not known existed.

She walked very slowly to the bus stop, her need to get home strong. Only when completely alone could she piece together the disjointed sentences, the breathlessly gasped words he had said, pausing now and then to drift into an exhausted sleep, a sleep from which, in the end, he had not awakened.

She needed quietness to understand and remember all that he had told her—but she bit her lip as she wondered how she could ever accept it all.

'Mia!' a voice called. It was Ian, running to her side. 'Darling, I was waiting in the café—I thought you would never come.'

She looked at him, but suddenly he was a stranger. Yet a brave man, for he had overcome his fear of illness to come to her side. But why had he ever left her? that inner voice of hers asked. Gideon Eastwood would never have left her alone to face the horror she had just endured.

'He's dead,' she said dully.

'Oh no!' Ian sounded shocked. 'My poor Mia!' He took her arm and without saying a word, led her to where he had parked the car. Vaguely she noticed that he was wrapping a rug round her, closing the window of the car, but it was all so distant she hardly realised what he was doing. She sat quietly while he drove her home.

Once he spoke: 'You can't stay there alone, Mia. Come back with me.'

She shivered. 'I'd rather go home, Ian. I'll have Nanny Evans.'

'I'm supposed to be speaking at the Club tonight,' Ian said worriedly, 'but I could postpone it—'

'Please don't, Ian,' she said. 'I'd—I'd rather not talk tonight.'

'You're sure?' She thought she heard relief in his voice. How brave of him to risk having to

38

cope with the tears she knew she would soon be shedding, she thought.

'Sure!'

She was glad when he left her at the vicarage door—Nanny Evans, who had always called herself, 'General Dogsbody,' for after being Mia's nanny, she had stayed on as housekeeper—opened it, her voice sharp, betraying her fear more than tears would have done.

'I hope you gave that foolish man of ours a scolding, Miss Mia, that I do. Walking with his head in the clouds as usual, I don't doubt . . .' she began. Then she stopped abruptly as she saw Mia's face. 'Oh, my child . . .' she exclaimed, opening her arms, enfolding Mia in them tightly, as she had so often done in the past.

Mrs. Evans pushed the front door shut and led Mia to the warm kitchen where the firelight glowed and sparked cheerfully, making the copper saucepans warmly bright, pushing Mia gently into a chair, producing a quick cup of strong sweet tea, then sitting by her side, holding Mia's cold hands.

'Tell me, childie,' Mrs. Evans said gently.

Mia tried to, stumbling with the words, tears sliding down her cheeks, trying to think carefully, to remember that there was so much she could not tell Nanny Evans, Ian, or anyone. At last she escaped to bed, pretending to swallow the sleeping pill she had been given.

She had to stay awake and plan. She had to know what she was going to do before Ian came next day.

At last she was alone, the door closed, the room's black emptiness pressing against her. She tried to remember what he had said. 'You are not my child, Mia . . .'

Those had been his first words. His voice, tired and sad.

'Not your child?' she whispered. 'But— Mummy . . .'

'Was not your mother, either.'

She had stared down at his unhappy face and felt his fingers stir in her hand. 'But we loved you so—much, so very much, Mia darling,' he had added.

'But—but why—my own parents . . .' The words had tumbled out of her mouth as she tried to accept what she knew must be the truth.

'Mia, we were married for fifteen years and, despite our prayers, God sent us no child. Our hearts were nearly broken until one day He sent you to us . . .' He had paused, his voice barely a whisper. 'It was in Spain.'

'Spain? Am I Spanish?' Mia had asked, thinking of her fair hair and light skin.

He had smiled wearily. 'Let me tell it my way, Mia. Your parents were both English. We were in Spain. I had had a breakdown and we were on holiday. The priest was my friend, he knew our problem—that we had no child. One day he came and said he had a child for me. Your mother was a child of seventeen herself. Her parents were angry when she eloped with the man she loved; they found her, had the marriage annulled, took the girl to Spain to have the baby secretly . . . They had persuaded her that it would be best for the child to be adopted.'

Mia had known pain, such terrible heart-aching pain as she had never known before. Her mother had rejected her, had given her away, like an unwanted toy.

The sick man had said softly: 'Don't judge her. She was so young. She wanted to do the right thing, but her parents were domineering. She wept . . .'

'And yet she gave me away,' Mia had cried out.

It was later that he went on: 'Have you ever wondered why we called you Mia?' he asked. 'I shall never forget when we went to the convent to fetch you. A girl was sobbing, terrible sobs. We could hear her voice, she spoke in English. "But it's my baby," she kept saying. "My baby—mine!" Then we heard her father's voice, indulgent, stem, persuasive. "You want your baby to have the best life, my dear. This is the only way." Then more tears. My wife and I nearly fled. She cried, too. When you were brought to us, I'll never forget my wife's face. She was so happy. We had waited fifteen years for you.'

41

He had paused then, drifting off into a restless sleep, and she had sat there, trying to accept the fact that he was not her father. That her real mother had been only seventeen—had wept over her.

Then her father had wakened and had said: 'Your mother has never forgotten you, Mia. Every birthday a special present came. We used to tell you it was from your godmother. Remember?'

She had remembered. On her last birthday an exotically beautiful silk stole had come. Oddly enough, she had never wondered about the strange godmother who sent no address or word with the present.

'That was why we called you Mia,' he had gone on, his thoughts drifting. ' "She's mine," your mother had cried. We were in Spain and so we called you Mia.'

'Why are you telling me now?' she had asked.

His face had been sad. 'Because, child, we must try to find your mother. I did not realise until recently how much a good family means to the Yates. This is something that might come to light in future years and it could only cause you trouble and distress. They might accuse you of hiding the truth. We must trace your mother and father and then tell the Yates ...'

'I can't see that it matters,' Mia told him. 'You'll always be my parents in my eyes.'

He had smiled. 'But to them, birth is important. I went to ask God for guidance this morning—for it is not easy to tell a beloved daughter that she is not your child . . .' His voice trailed away sadly.

She had wept then, kissing his hand, assuring him she would always call him her father. That they would forget. . . But he had not agreed. He told her that he always kept the stamps from the mysterious birthday parcels.

'Your mother has travelled all over the world, but for the last three years she has lived in one of the islands of the Seychelles. We'll see when your next birthday present comes what the postmark is and start enquiries there.' The stamps, he had told her, were in a drawer of his desk.

'Shall I tell Ian?' she asked.

He looked worried. 'Not yet, Mia. Let's have something constructive to tell him. I'm afraid that if the Yates found out, they would make Ian give you up.'

'And Ian would let them?' she asked.

He sighed. 'Ian is not a strong character, Mia. I often wonder if . . .' He paused. 'No, it must be your decision. Marry him—if you love him enough.' Again he paused, and she had seen what an effort he found it to talk.

But he went on, 'We must conduct our investigation discreetly, Mia. Your mother is only thirty-seven now—perhaps her husband, her friends see her as a young woman. It might spoil her whole life—her happiness. Her husband might not know she had once had a child, or her children might resent the news. Your mother might be an actress. It could ruin her career . . .'

'But she must remember me to send me a present,' Mia had said.

He had nodded. 'That is so. I might be wrong. Perhaps she longs to tell you the truth but has given her word not to do so. But, Mia, let us tread gently. I don't want anyone hurt.'

But I'm hurt, Mia had wanted to cry out. Hurt terribly. And then she had remembered the seventeen-year-old girl who had sobbed, 'But she's my baby, mine.' Perhaps her mother had promised not to tell her child the truth? Perhaps . . .

Mia's thoughts skidded to a standstill and she was back again in the cold, dark, lonely room. She switched on the light, slid out of bed, pushing her feet into mules, slipping on her dressing-gown. She went down the stairs cautiously, using a torch, not wanting to wake Nanny Evans. Once inside the study, she closed the door and switched on the light, leaning against the door.

She opened the drawer her father had told her about and found the envelope of carefully saved stamps. Three were clipped together. The postmark was hard to read, but at last she succeeded. It was a strange name . . . Isle d'Amour. The Isle of Love.

44

Would it be that for her? she wondered. Would she trace her real mother and be welcomed with open arms? Or would she find she must hold her tongue and slink away, knowing she was unwanted?

He had said they must wait for her birthday and the next parcel, that her mother might have moved again to another country.

Yet how could she wait? Mia asked herself. How could she bear to sit patiently when she wanted—when she needed—so urgently to find her real mother? Her mother who had wept when they were separated—who still loved her enough to send her a gift each year.

'But I promise not to tell anyone, Daddy darling,' Mia said gently. 'No matter what happens, I won't hurt my mother.'

CHAPTER THREE

Mia got off the bus at Ludgate Circus and began to walk towards St. Paul's. Every now and then, she glanced at the slip of paper in her hand and re-read the scribbled words: 'Maillard & Renaud, Shipbuilders, 15 St. Paul's Churchyard.'

Would they be able to help her? she wondered, remembering the words of the girl at the travel bureau.

'Isle d'Amour . . .?' she had repeated. 'No

45

one's ever gone there through us, though I have got the name of a guest-house. It's a quiet place, you know, mostly oldies, retired types. Fabulous, of course, always sunshine, but terribly boring.'

Mia had tried not to show impatience, but had wondered why everything had to be so difficult. After that first terrible night, the night her father—for he would always be that to her—had died, she had been frantic with the need to escape from everyone, for the sympathy and kindness only made the desolation more real. Ian, the Yates, even Nanny Evans had made it worse. Ian had finally accepted it, when Mia lied, telling him she wanted to visit some old friends of her father's who lived on the Isle d'Amour.

'I must get away, Ian,' she had said. He must have recognised the desperation in her voice.

'So long as you're back in time for our wedding, darling,' he had said.

The Yates had agreed. 'It might be wise, Mia.'

Her father's solicitor had been most helpful, letting her have a substantial advance on the money she would inherit. She had to tell him she was adopted, in case it affected the will, but he had known and the will had been drawn up accordingly. 'He made me promise never to tell a soul.'

Everything, but everything, seemed to go wrong, Mia thought, as she shivered in the chilly travel bureau, even spring had somehow got lost on the way and the weather was still bitterly cold.

'There's a post office on the island, so surely boats must call in with mail?' Mia said as patiently as she could.

'I think they're often flown in, but there are freight boats. A few cruising liners call there . . .' The girl had looked through some papers and found the name of a liner that would reach the island in two months' time. 'You could go by sea and wait at Mombasa, or fly out . . .'

Ma's cold fingers beat an impatient tattoo on the desk. 'I must get there soon. I can't wait,' she had said.

Once again, it was perhaps the desperation in her voice that helped solve her problem, for the girl had scribbled a name on a piece of paper.

'Try this firm,' she said kindly. 'They have business on the island and frequently fly out by their own plane and sometimes give people lifts. Let me know the date and I'll book your flight to Mombasa. You want me to book you in at the guest-house?'

'Oh, please,' Mia said, clutching the note as if it was a lifeline. 'I'm staying at the Regent Palace. I'll get in touch,' she had added, almost running from the travel bureau, fearful lest the girl want to talk.

Walking up the hill, Mia looked at the tall

47

skyscraper that seemed to gaze down insolently on the cathedral. She took a deep breath, said a little prayer, and went into the building. If only they could help her!

Waiting for the lift, she straightened the skirt of her oatmeal-coloured suit and looked in an obliging mirror. Her eyes did not look like her eyes any more, they seemed to have sunk in her face, and her old look of happiness had gone.

Nanny Evans had said sadly, 'It'll come back, childie.' She had added, 'Don't fret too much—your dad wouldn't have liked it, you know that.'

'Oh, Dad . . . Dad,' Mia thought miserably, as the lift door slid open and swallowed her up.

She got out on the tenth floor and walked along the corridor to the glass door. 'Maillard & Renaud,' she read, and went inside.

She found herself staring down a long narrow room with desks on either side of the centre aisle. The typewriters were hammering away, several phone bells shrilled impatiently and she shuddered slightly, thinking how she would hate this sort of work. The girls went on typing, but stared curiously at her. The receptionist, a girl with shoulder-length red hair, was friendly, but looked about fifteen.

Mia explained the reason she was there. 'I don't know who I ought to see,' she finished.

The girl glanced at the clock. 'Are you in an

48

awful hurry?'

'I'm afraid so,' Mia confessed.

The girl sighed a little. 'I'll see if he's free.' She hurried down the aisle and in a few moments was back. 'Please follow me. I'm terribly sorry, but I forgot to ask your name.'

Mia told her and the girl smiled. 'You must think me awfully daft, but I'm new here and always making mistakes which makes me nervous, so I make more. I hope I'm doing the right thing, but Miss Vaughan, she's the P.A. and is rather . . .'

Mia smiled reassuringly. 'I'm sure it's all right, for I did tell you it was urgent.'

The girl opened a glass door, stood back and announced, 'Miss Barton, Mr. Eastwood.'

Even as Mia stepped into the luxuriously furnished room, her heart seemed to skip a beat. Mr. Eastwood? It couldn't be! It couldn't possibly be . . . Mia thought wildly. There must be more than one Mr. Eastwood in London. There couldn't be such a coincidence as . . . But there was. The big man who stood up behind the huge mahogany desk was staring at her, his eyes focused on her with the same strangely searching look that had made her feel so uncomfortable on the night of her engagement party.

'Well . . .!' Gideon Eastwood said, and she saw amusement as well as surprise in his eyes. 'What brings you here?'

She wanted to turn and flee. This man,

whose face she had slapped! This man, who had been so insultingly rude, accusing her of marrying Ian for his money. And who had insulted Ian also, calling him weak and a 'mother's boy'.

Gideon moved first. He came to her side, taking her arm, leading her to an armchair, gently pushing her into it. 'Have you lost your tongue?' he teased. 'That's a change. I can't imagine this being a social call—or did our mutual friend, Ian Yates, send you here?'

She managed to find her voice. 'I didn't know it was you,' she said. She knew he did not believe her.

She knew from the way he smiled, from the way he said: 'Well, then this is a double surprise. Who did you expect to see here? I happen to be the managing director and the girl told me someone was urgently needing a lift to the Isle d'Amour.'

She moistened her lips nervously. 'Yes, I do. I went to a travel bureau in Shaftesbury Avenue and they sent me to you. There's no liner calling in for two months and I simply must get there before that . . .' She heard the note of urgency in her voice and twisted her hands together, trying to calm herself. But why, oh why, she was thinking miserably, had it to be Gideon Eastwood from whom she must ask a favour?

'Why do you want to go to Isle d'Amour?' he asked, his voice cold.

Mia twisted her fingers together. If only she could tell him the truth—that she had to go there to find her mother, her real mother, the mother who had wept when she had to give her baby away, who loved her enough to remember to send a birthday present each year. Yet the truth could not be told, Mia knew that. Her father, as she still thought of him, had made her understand. First, Mia must find her mother, then decide whether it was wise to tell her the truth or not.

Mia looked up, tilting her chin defiantly. 'I think that's my business.'

He smiled. 'I'm afraid you're wrong there.' There was an ominous quietness in his voice that frightened her—it was as if he held the weapon that could destroy her, and he knew it. 'You see, it happens to be my business. We, on the island, are very particular . . .'

Mia interrupted him. 'Is it your island? I mean, where you live?' she asked, catching her breath with dismay. It would have to happen this way! Why must he be involved? It would make her search twice as hard, she thought.

'I told you I lived on an island in the Indian Ocean,' he reminded her, 'or haven't you realised yet that the Seychelles are in the Indian Ocean?'

She felt her cheeks burn. The truth was, she hadn't! She had looked at the map, seen the Seychelles were off the coast of Africa, but that was all. 'No,' she said honestly, 'I hadn't.'

He leaned back, folding his arms in the arrogant way she disliked and looking down his aquiline nose at her. 'To continue, and please—' he added, glancing at his wrist watch, 'no interruptions this time. I'm a very busy man.'

She was tempted to jump up and walk from the room, but her need for his help was too urgent, so she folded her hands and waited, pretending a meekness she did not feel.

'To return, we are very particular as to who comes on the island. There are questions to be answered: how long do you plan to stay? Do you intend to settle there? Have you any idea of the kind of place it is? Do you plan to work there? What do you do to earn a living? If I arrange the lift for you, it means I am sponsoring you and can therefore be held responsible. Now d'you understand why it's my business?' He paused, his voice losing its slightly amused, almost patronising tone and becoming stern. 'I cannot contemplate arranging a lift unless you are prepared to answer my questions.'

Mia drew a long deep breath, strengthening her back, lifting her chin. 'I wish to stay on the island for two or three months,' she said. 'I do not intend to settle there. I know that the island is long and narrow, that the maximum temperature is eighty-four and the minimum seventy-seven. I know there are palm trees and coral and that many of the inhabitants are retired people. I am a trained nursery school teacher . . .' She paused, seeing the surprise he instantly controlled on his face. 'But I have plenty of money with which to support myself.'

He smiled. 'Well, very adroitly handled, Miss Barton. You should be in the diplomatic corps. You have answered all my questions and told me precisely nothing. What does your fiancé have to say to all this? I understood you were to be married quite soon?'

'In just over five months' time,' Mia said calmly. 'He thinks it's a good idea.'

Gideon Eastwood's eyes narrowed. 'And your father?'

She tried to keep her voice steady. 'He's dead.'

The room seemed filled with a silence that was almost unbearable and then Gideon was by her side, holding her hands tightly, bending down, his face concerned.

'I am sorry. I had no idea. How did it happen?' He pulled a chair close and sat near her, his hands holding hers as he leaned forward.

Mia told him, but she found it difficult to speak as her throat kept tightening. She tried not to look at him, but his grey eyes had an almost magnetic influence on her. She did not realise that she was clinging tightly to his hands, but she did know that it was as if a warm current of strength flowed down his arms, through their hands into her body. It was a strength that slowly filled her, giving her control of her voice and tears, and an amazing feeling of comfort. For the first time since her father's death, she did not feel alone.

'Why didn't you tell me at once?' Gideon asked. She gave a little shrug. 'Somehow I thought everyone knew.'

'I wish I had known,' he said gravely. 'Just after we met, I flew to Paris; from there I went to New York and I only got back last night . . . I do wish I'd known.'

A knock came on the door as it opened. 'I'm so sorry, Mr. Eastwood,' a feminine, authoritative voice said. 'I told that stupid girl you were to see no one except by appointment . . .'

As Gideon released Mia's hands, she turned to see an incredibly beautiful girl standing in the door, frowning. A tall slender girl with dark hair casually but obviously expensively curled round her head. She stood with the same arrogant ease Mia had noticed in Gideon Eastwood. The girl wore a simple grey suit so elegantly cut that it screamed its cost. Her dark eyes flashed with anger.

Mia automatically stood up. 'It was not the girl's fault,' she said with simple dignity. 'She wanted to wait and ask you—you are Miss Vaughan, I imagine?' Without knowing it, Mia was talking with assurance, determined not to let the young red-headed girl be blamed for what was her fault. 'I said it was very urgent and that I had an appointment to keep, so she came to ask Mr. Eastwood if he could see me. But it was not her fault. If there is a fault,' she added, 'it was mine.'

Miss Vaughan's face looked flushed. Perhaps, Mia thought, Miss Vaughan was like Gideon Eastwood, so accustomed to people being scared of them that if you showed courage, they were surprised.

'It was not the girl's fault,' Mia repeated yet once more.

'I am Miss Vaughan, but the girl knew that we make rules to protect Mr. Eastwood and they should be kept. He can't just be seen by anyone . . .'

Mia smiled. 'The riff-raff? You're so right, but . . .'

Gideon spoke then for the first time. He had been watching the two girls, surprised, and looking a little amused, at the gallant way Mia had leapt to the defence of the red-headed girl. 'In any case, Miss Barton happens to be a friend of mine,' he said quietly.

Gwyneth Vaughan looked at him and dismay replaced the anger. 'I'm sorry, I didn't realise . . . I didn't mean to be rude.'

Gideon smiled. 'On the contrary, my dear conscientious Gwyneth,' he said, opening the door and waiting for her to walk out, 'you were only doing your duty.'

Closing the door, he looked at Mia. 'My Girl Friday or personal assistant, as she prefers to be called. I often wonder how I'd manage without her, but there are times when she acts like a watchdog, or worse still, like a possessive mother smothering her child with protection.'

Even as Mia smiled, she was thinking that it was not motherly love that had shone on Miss Vaughan's face. Nor was it the desire to protect a child that had made Miss Vaughan's eyes flash with suspicion. Obviously Miss Vaughan was in love with Gideon Eastwood. Mia wondered if he knew. Probably he did. It was the sort of thing that would amuse him.

She sat down, looking worried. 'I do hope that nice red-headed girl won't get into trouble. She told me she was new and kept making mistakes. I'm afraid I was very insistent about being seen . . .'

Gideon sat down behind the desk and scribbled a note on a pad. 'I'll see she doesn't,' he promised. 'Are you really in a hurry?'

Mia nodded. 'I'm meeting Ian for tea at the Savoy.'

Gideon frowned. 'When do you want to go to the Isle d'Amour?'

'As soon as possible.'

'What do Ian's people think of that rather fantastic escape from reality?' Gideon asked, the sarcastic note that was seldom far away creeping back into his voice.

'They think it's because—' Mia began, and stopped. He had nearly trapped her into the truth. Her face burned. 'They think I want to go there and grieve.'

'I hope you won't,' Gideon said sternly. 'It's the last thing your father would wish.'

'I know. I just—just want to be alone for a while.'

'The island isn't a desert island, you know. There are people there. Mostly retired or people escaping from reality because they can't face up to life.' He paused. 'Have you booked at the guest house?'

'The travel bureau are doing that.'

'Good. It's run by a very nice couple. There'll be no night life on the island, you know—dancing, etcetera.'

'I know.' The palms of her hands were damp as she wondered if he was deliberately taunting her and then, at the end, would tell her he could not help her.

He scribbled something on his pad. 'Are you still in Hawbridge?'

'No. I had to leave, for the new vicar is moving in. I'm at the Regent Palace.'

He frowned. 'Alone?'

Quick angry resentment rose inside her. Why must he always harp on her youth? 'Of course I'm alone! I'm nearly twenty and . . .'

He smiled, looking for a second like a mischievous boy. 'How you do bite,' he teased. 'I wasn't referring to your youth, which so obviously riles you. I only wondered if you had relatives with you.'

Mia stood up. 'I must be wasting your

time, Mr. Eastwood,' she said stiffly, as disappointment flooded her. 'I quite understand ...'

He looked at her oddly. 'Do you? Somehow I don't think you do. Give me the name of the travel bureau and I'll arrange everything,' he said crisply. 'I imagine you have a passport, being vaccinated, and so on?'

Mia stared at him. He spoke as to a stranger, but that did not worry her as the warmth of relief swept over her.

'You will take me? Oh, thank you. Yes, I've a passport, everything.'

'Good.' He wrote down the particulars she gave him and then led the way to the door. 'You'll get forty-eight hours' notice, but not more.'

She was being quietly hustled out of the room, but she turned. 'Can I give you a cheque now?'

He frowned impatiently. 'What on earth for?'

'The flight from Mombasa to the island.'

'We don't run commercial flights,' he said coldly. 'We only give friends—or people in dire straits—a lift. Goodbye.' He closed the door before she could speak.

She stared at it, wondering if he saw her as a friend or as someone in dire straits! She decided it must be the latter.

She walked down the room past the typists and the red-headed girl gave her a quick friendly smile. As Mia walked along the corridor towards the lift, she heard the sharp staccato sounds of high-heeled shoes. She turned. Miss Vaughan was almost running, her face worried.

'I wanted to apologise, Miss Barton. I didn't realise you were a friend of Gideon's.'

Gideon, Mia thought. In the office, it had been Mr. Eastwood! 'It's quite all right,' Mia told her. 'I realise how busy he is.'

'He's an amazing man, Miss Barton. Brilliant, makes quick decisions, the kindest man in the world,' Miss Vaughan said. Mia wanted to yawn rudely. She was so wholeheartedly tired of hearing Gideon Eastwood's praises always sung! 'So many people impose on his kindness,' the beautiful Gwyneth Vaughan went on, 'so I must protect him.'

She smiled and glanced pointedly at Mia's left hand where the ruby ring Ian had given her shone. 'You know how it is, Miss Barton, when you care for someone. Was he able to help you? I gather it was urgent?'

Mia hesitated. Miss Vaughan was pumping her, and not very diplomatically. What did it matter? Probably Gideon would ask Miss Vaughan to arrange the flights. 'I wanted a lift to the Isle d'Amour,' she said.

Miss Vaughan's face darkened, as if a cloud had passed over the sun, threatening bad weather ahead. Her dark eyes narrowed. 'You want to go to the island?' she said, sounding shocked, as if Mia was contemplating something terrible. 'Its name is most misleading.' Then she smiled. 'Your honeymoon?'

'No. I'm not getting married yet awhile.' Mia hesitated. 'You've been to the island?' she asked.

Gwyneth Vaughan smiled. 'I frequently go with Gideon. He has a beautiful home there, but he never entertains.'

'I'm afraid I've an appointment,' Mia said, beginning to walk to the lift.

Miss Vaughan walked with her. 'It's very quiet on the island,' she said. 'You'll be bored.'

The lift came, the doors slid open. As Mia stepped in, Miss Vaughan's last words came through the sliding door as it closed: 'I should think carefully about going, Miss Barton. I'm afraid you may be very unhappy there.'

Mia was not sure if it was a warning or a plea. Suddenly she wanted to laugh. Could Miss Vaughan be jealous?

*   *   *

Mia was ready for the flight long before the ticket reached her at the hotel. She had packed, having shopped carefully, remembering the hot days that awaited her, hating the small impersonal bedroom, the difficult meetings with Ian who, although he

60

had proved surprisingly sympathetic, kept saying how much he would miss her.

'So long as I know you'll come back,' he said miserably, as he drove her to the airport.

'Of course I will,' Mia said, but sometimes she wondered if she should be frank with him now, and admit that she was no longer sure that she loved him or wanted to be Mrs. Ian Yates.

Gideon Eastwood's words had opened her eyes and forced her to admit the truth, that whatever decision Ian made would always have to be referred to the Yates first.

Yet as he kissed her, she had not the heart to hurt him with the truth. Perhaps while she was away, he would stop loving her so much, would realise she was not a suitable wife for him, she thought.

'I loathe farewells, Mia,' Ian said with a violence that surprised her. 'D'you mind if I don't wait and wave goodbye?'

'Of course not,' she said, but she felt very much alone after he had gone.

She walked down the aisle to her seat as the plane filled up. There was an empty seat by her. Was that Gideon Eastwood's? she wondered, and wished someone else could sit by her side, for she felt miserable and in no mood to cope with his sarcastic arrogance.

What a strange mixture he was, she thought unhappily. He could be so kind—as when he learned of her father's death—and so cruelly cold.

Suddenly a strange fear possessed her. She knew she was doing the wrong thing. This was a terrible mistake. She must get out of the plane . . .

She began to gather her things hastily and had half-stood when a hand touched her shoulder.

'Everything under control?' Gideon Eastwood enquired, and Mia jumped with surprise, her handbag sliding out of her hand, flying open, so that her powder compact, lipstick, eyebrow pencil, purse, keys, shot across the floor.

'Oh, goodness!' Mia cried, her face bright red as she bent down, and Gideon must have moved at the same moment and, with a resounding crack, their heads met. 'Oh!' she cried out with pain, sitting back, rubbing her head ruefully.

A husky-voiced blonde air hostess came hurrying. 'Don't worry, sir,' she said to Gideon Eastwood. 'I'll pick everything up.'

But the big, broad-shouldered man did not listen. He was on his knees, picking each item up separately, dropping it in Mia's lap with that supercilious look on his face she hated so much.

'Better check you've got everything,' he said curtly. 'That is, if you know what rubbish you've got.'

Mia heard a subdued chuckle and knew that

the other passengers were watching with amused eyes. She was horribly aware that her little green hat had been pushed on one side, that her cheeks were scarlet. She bundled everything into her handbag.

'Thank you,' she murmured.

Gideon stood up, dusting the knees of his dark grey suit. How completely masculine he looked, even in the most elegant clothes, Mia thought, absurdly annoyed by his perfection.

'I'm sorry,' she said.

His face was cold and unfriendly. 'Not at all. It could happen to anyone. I hope you won't find the trip too tiring. See you in Mombasa,' he added, and walked down the aisle.

She caught her breath. Surely that was a snub, she thought. She had dreaded his company, yet now that she knew he was sitting far down the plane, it was as if he had slapped her face in revenge.

He was opening a briefcase, spreading papers out before him. Perhaps he had wanted to sit alone so that he could work and not waste time talking. She wondered who had booked the tickets. Gwyneth Vaughan, no doubt. Suddenly Mia began to laugh. Had Gwyneth deliberately arranged this, separating them, probably saying to Gideon that it would be a more pleasant flight for him if he travelled alone?

Mia was still laughing when the seat next to her was taken. 'What's the joke?' a friendly voice asked.

Mia looked round and saw that her companion was a red-headed man. His hair was cut so short she could just see it was sandy, but she knew from the freckles that covered his face what colour his hair was. He was a short, lightly-built man, in his early twenties, she guessed.

'Nothing, really,' she confessed, and began to laugh again.

It seemed so utterly absurd if it was true. How could Gwyneth Vaughan, that gorgeous if icy-eyed beauty, be jealous of her? Mia wondered. It must be her imagination. Yet if you loved someone, you could think crazy things. And Mia was sure of one thing— Gwyneth Vaughan was deeply in love with her boss, Gideon Eastwood.

It was as if her laughter had created a bond between Mia and her companion. They exchanged names. He was Toby Caldecoot, he said. She learned that he, too, was going to the Seychelles, but to the island called Mahé.

'Isle d'Amour,' he repeated as she told him her destination. 'Boy, oh boy, it sounds quite a place,' he added, his hazel eyes twinkling at her. 'Maybe I'll come and visit you one day.'

She realised that she had hardly noticed that the plane had taken off and they were already high above the big cotton-wool clouds, in that perfect colourless sky that seemed so pure.

She was surprised how swiftly the flight passed. They had so much to talk about and Toby was a good listener as well as an interesting speaker. It was only when they all slept that Mia, waking up and unable to sleep again, knew the fear that had made her try to leave the plane before it took off, and caused that embarrassing moment when Gideon had touched her and she had dropped her handbag! Once again, despair and loneliness swept through her. This was a crazy thing she had done, she thought unhappily. How would she ever find her mother without even the smallest clue? If only her father, as she still thought of him, had lived. He could have given her the name of the town in Spain—perhaps they could have traced the priest.

But how, on an island, could she trace her mother when she had given her word not to let anyone know the truth? Mia wondered. They would make 'enquiries', her father had said, but how did you make them when you hadn't anything to tell them?

If only she could have told Gideon Eastwood, asked his advice, she thought miserably. She glanced down the aisle. He was asleep, arms folded, completely relaxed. Of course he would sleep just as efficiently as he did everything else. He was so perfect it just wasn't true, she thought rebelliously, and then wondered at the strength of her annoyance with him. Why had he the power to make her so angry? He couldn't possibly be as perfect as he appeared to be—or as people said he was.

Suddenly she remembered something her father had said: 'We're all human, Mia. Each of us has his Achilles' heel.'

So if her father was right, and he always had been, she thought lovingly, even Gideon Eastwood must have an Achilles' heel. She wondered what it was.

She slept fitfully until the plane began to come to life and Toby's jokes and laughter stopped her from thinking worriedly about the problem that lay ahead of her.

She was surprised when they arrived. Toby walked with her to the Customs. The air was warm, caressingly so on her cheeks, the sky a bright blue, the sun dazzling.

'Thanks for a fabulous trip, Mia,' Toby said, holding her hand tightly and smiling at her. 'I'll see you again.'

'Thank you,' Mia said, emphasising the last word. 'I really enjoyed the flight,' she said honestly, knowing how worried and unhappy she would have been without his friendly companionship.

He still held her hand. 'Good,' he said, and hesitated as if there was something he wanted to say. Almost casually he lifted her left hand, glancing at the huge ruby and then smiled at her. 'I hope you have a good holiday.'

He waved as he went off and she turned to look for one of the Customs' officials, but

Gideon was by her side.

'Go and sit down, Mia,' he said curtly. 'I'll cope with this. Give me your keys.'

Mia hesitated. She could manage quite well, she was about to say, she wasn't a child, but then she glanced up at his face and saw that his mouth was a thin line, his face white with controlled anger. Now what had upset him? she wondered. People were milling round everywhere, too many curious eyes, she thought, and she didn't fancy another scene, so she meekly handed him her keys and went to sit down on a bench against the wall.

She yawned and shivered when Gideon shook her gently, blinking up at him sleepily.

'Tired?' he asked curtly.

She stood up. 'A bit.'

'Won't be long,' he told her.

A long white car awaited them, a uniformed chauffeur stacked their suitcases and drove them to a big modern hotel. Vaguely Mia saw white modern buildings rubbing shoulders with squalid-looking tin shanties, a sprawling mass of traffic that crawled with noisy impatience, bicycles, scooters, crowds of strange-looking people on the pavements, but the sleepiness was too much for her and again she dozed and Gideon had to wake her at the hotel.

He led her inside and up to a room on the fifth floor. 'I'll ring you later and we'll have something to eat,' he said curtly. 'Have a bath and sleep.'

She did what he had told her to—but only, she told herself, because it was what she wanted to do! It was bliss to soak in the hot scented water, to creep under a cool sheet on the bed and let sleep overcome her.

The shrill cry of the phone awakened her. She was yawning as she answered it. 'Be ready in fifteen minutes,' Gideon said curtly. 'I'll wait in the hall.'

She yawned and blinked at her watch. Had she really slept so long? She showered to try to waken herself, then dressed quickly in a white sheath frock, white shoes, choosing an emerald green necklace and earrings. She made up faster than she had ever done before, brushing her hair back from her face, fastening it with pins.

Gideon was waiting in the hall. He looked at her without comment. He had obviously just showered too, for his short dark hair glistened with water. He wore a cream seersucker suit, immaculately tailored.

In the dining-room, the head waiter nearly fell over, walking backwards with obsequious politeness as he escorted them to a reserved table. Four waiters hovered as Gideon ordered the meal and also wine, without consulting her, Mia noticed resentfully.

It was a strange meal, for although all round them was the hum of laughter and conversation, they ate in silence, Mia growing more uncomfortable as each moment passed.

She searched her mind for a way in which to start a conversation, but looking at his forbidding frown, she hesitated. It was absurd, but she felt like a schoolgirl hauled before the headmaster to be scolded, for Gideon positively emanated an aura of disapproval. Therefore the attack did not surprise her when it came. But the subject of it did.

Over coffee, Gideon unexpectedly lifted her left hand and looked at her engagement ring.

'I thought you must have broken your engagement.'

'B-b-broken my—' Mia stammered.

His grey eyes were cold. 'From your behaviour on the plane, I thought you had either forgotten Ian or broken off the engagement,' Gideon said slowly, as if explaining something very elementary to a child, Mia thought.

'My—my behaviour?'

The hum of laughter and voices went on, the soft bustle of waiters round them seemed to intensify the quiet animosity in Gideon's voice. 'Was it necessary,' he asked, 'to make such a spectacle of yourself on the plane, flirting so outrageously with a stranger?'

'Stranger?' Mia repeated.

Gideon lost his temper. 'Good grief, girl,' he exploded, his voice still controlled and quiet but so full of anger she shivered, 'must you echo every word? You're an engaged girl and yet you . . .'

The penny dropped and Mia understood. Puzzlement replaced by anger, she said quickly: 'Because a girl is engaged, it doesn't mean she can't speak to a man.'

'There are ways of speaking,' he said sarcastically. 'Or haven't you learned that yet? You deliberately encouraged him. I hope he doesn't follow you to our island.'

Mia was fighting her anger and her cheeks felt red-hot. 'He may visit me,' she said coldly.

'Oh no! That'll be the end!' Gideon said, frowning.

Trembling, Mia bit her lip. 'You . . . you are utterly and completely impossible,' she said, her voice unsteady. 'Toby helped me enjoy what could have been a long miserable flight. I . . . I was—' she paused, fighting for control. 'I felt very much alone, and Toby made me laugh. He knows I'm engaged, and I think he has a girlfriend in Mahé.'

'How very interesting. Maybe you'd like to change your mind and go to Mahé where people of your type can be found. You'll be bored to tears on Isle d'Amour.'

Mia felt her control was going and she could take no more so she stood up. 'Mr. Eastwood,' she said very quietly, 'you were good enough to say you'd give me a lift to the island. Once I'm there, I promise you I won't bother you any more. Can we leave it at that and stop bickering?'

Gideon stood up, beckoning a waiter with

the flick of a finger. 'I couldn't agree more. I, too, am weary of this fruitless discussion. Be ready at nine in the morning. I'll arrange for dinner to be served in your room.' His voice was very formal and stiff. 'I regret that I can't show you the sights of Mombasa, but I have business to do. I wouldn't advise you to go out alone. You need a good night's rest and then you may regain your manners.'

He took her arm, stalking to the lift with her, and left her after pressing the button. She watched him stride to the desk and speak to the clerk.

She hesitated. It would be pleasant to wander round the town, but she was very tired and she could only make a fool of herself, get into a mess and have to be rescued by a triumphant Gideon, which would make her life even more unbearable than it was at this moment!

In her room she went to the window and gazed out. It was all so different, so very different from what she was used to . . . She leant her hot face against the glass. If only, she thought, it was Toby Caldecoot giving her a lift to the Isle d'Amour. If only it could be anyone—anyone but Gideon Eastwood!

CHAPTER FOUR

The flight to the island was uneventful except for the fact that Gideon seemed to have completely forgotten his anger and was surprisingly friendly.

Standing in the dripping heat of the airport, Mia saw how everyone leapt to obey his slightest wish, but as he settled himself behind the controls of the private plane, and turned to smile reassuringly at her, she began to understand a little of the reasons people so respected him. He seemed to throw out an air of self-confidence and efficiency.

She knew no fear at all on the flight. She looked down at the deep strange colour of the Indian Ocean. They were flying above an island now and the water near the land was a different shade and absolutely transparent. She felt excited for the first time—excited because the first lap of her search for her mother was over. Soon she would be on the island and the search would go on until she finally traced her real mother, the mother she had to find.

'This is us,' Gideon said cheerfully.

From their height, the island looked just as the girl at the travel bureau had said—long and very narrow. Now as they circled it and went down lower, she could pick out items—

coves with white sand, lagoons, yachts rocking, dark clumps of trees. A town with jetties running out to sea, fishing boats, a huge mountain, houses clustered round the harbour. Now the earth was racing up to meet them and Mia caught her breath. She glanced at Gideon and he was whistling softly, his face happy and relaxed. It made her relax, and when the plane landed with barely the gentlest of a bump, she realised that, for the first time, she had not been afraid of landing.

There was a wide tarmac strip and several hangars from which some men came running.

Gideon looked at her. 'Don't worry if you feel giddy. It's normal procedure,' he told her.

The soft warm air touched her cheeks gently. She looked round her wonderingly. Everywhere there were palm trees—but not one was straight; they were all slanted in the same direction. But there were other trees, huge trunks with wide branches, bright with red flowers and green leaves.

She saw on a road something that looked almost comical, for it was so out of place near the modern plane. An old-fashioned carriage with the hood down, it was painted black, but the cushions in it were deep red. The white horse stood patiently, flicking his tail at the flies, and on his head was a comical little straw hat.

Even as she looked, a man climbed down and limped towards them. He was short, very thin and bald, his skin burned dark brown by the sun.

'Eee, sir,' he greeted Gideon with a smile that seemed to fill his puck-like face. 'I tell ee we war mighty afear'd you'd not come. A bad storm it was earlier.'

Gideon smiled. 'I know. We missed it, fortunately.' He glanced round. 'I don't see Mrs. Haseldine.'

'No, sir, nary do I,' the man replied. 'Was you expecting her?' His eyes had shifted to Mia who stood, lost in the beauty around her, the glimpse of a distant sandy bay with waves beating against rocks, mountains across the water, only hearing the conversation vaguely.

She jumped when Gideon spoke to her. 'You did say you'd booked in at the guest house?' he asked.

It took Mia a moment to understand and then she nodded. 'Of course. The girl at the travel bureau told me she had sent a cable.'

'You didn't bother to check if they could take you?'

'I didn't think it was necessary,' Mia began. 'The bureau had my address. If the guest house had . . .' but Gideon was not listening.

He glanced at his watch. 'Sometimes her horse is lame. We'll drop you off. Get in,' he said curtly.

Mia obeyed, thinking how comfortable the old-fashioned carriage was. As the horse walked down the narrow earth road, the trees intertwining overhead so that it was pleasantly cool, Mia asked Gideon: 'You don't have cars here?'

'Good grief, no,' he almost exploded. 'Not this side of the island. And we won't get any, if we can help it.'

The little man whistled cheerfully and the horse broke into a gentle trot. Mia sat back, and gazed at the beauty around her. If Gideon had remained the friendly man he had been on the plane she would have asked him a thousand questions, but instead she sat stiffly, trying to pretend he was not by her side.

The road twisted and then went slowly downhill towards the coast. Mia caught glimpses of deep blue water—of a tinkling waterfall, of bright orange flowers clambering over a rock—of rows of trees with huge red-petalled flowers. And everywhere the palm trees.

The carriage stopped outside a building that seemed to cling to the rocky ground, leaning over the lagoon. It was so calm, the blue water. The lagoon was circled by a reef of coral; far out, Mia could see the opening to the ocean and the white flecks of surf as the waves beat against the reef, throwing great sheets of water in the air which fell, scintillatingly beautiful, as the drops parted.

Gideon got out and went to knock on the door. The house was circular with a wide terrace on the ground floor, and a balcony above it. But every window was dark, shrouded by cotton blinds so that they looked like closed eyes. The house had a still ominous silence, and suddenly Mia shivered.

The fear that had hit her just before she left England returned. But this time it was a thousand times worse. Here she was, on an island in the Seychelles, thousands of miles from England, on what could probably be called a wild goose chase. Why had she been so impatient—why—why? she asked herself.

Gideon hammered louder and then walked round the side of the building. The funny little man called Pen, the horse's reins loosely in his hands, twisted to look at her with a friendly smile: 'Hope you'll be happy here, miss, that I do. 'Tis a real happy place and you wouldn't hear else.'

Mia wondered where she had heard that way of speaking—and remembered a holiday she had spent once with her father in Cornwall. 'You're from England?' she said.

The little man grinned, looking more than ever like one of Walt Disney's dwarfs.

'That I'm not, miss. I'm Cornish and I belong down there, but I've been out here many a year. The boss—' he jerked his head in the direction Gideon had vanished—'he's a good one, and that's no lie. I lost me job on the mines, for I got badly hurt in an accident there. Proper dead, I seemed, for days, and then when I got up no one'd look at me. I

76

couldn't walk or do naught, just sit and stare, and then—' his face lit up with his grin—'he brought me out here, and 'twas the sun what cured me.'

He paused and smiled again. 'Look, I couldn't do better 'twas I was a king, couldn't I? My own little house, a garden, my horse . . . this easy job and the grand old lady to talk to . . . and all 'cos of him . . .' He stopped abruptly and Mia saw that Gideon had returned.

'The house is locked up and empty. They must be away.' He tapped his foot angrily and looked at Mia.

She caught her breath with dismay. 'They're not there?'

'They're not just out shopping, if that's what you're hoping,' Gideon said curtly. 'Wait.' He turned to look across the road. Half-hidden by a line of palm trees was a group of thatched huts and a small boy came running. His brown face was bright with pleasure as he smiled up at Gideon, talking in a strange kind of French that Mia found it hard to understand.

She caught words—'husband—ill—Mahé'— so she was not so surprised when Gideon turned to her and said: 'Her husband was taken ill and they went to Mahé for an operation.' He frowned. 'But it's not like Phoebe. If she'd made your booking, she'd have arranged things.'

'I did make the booking,' Mia said in unexpected self-defence, feeling more and

77

more of a nuisance. What had she said to him at the hotel the other night? she asked herself. Wasn't it that once they reached the island, she would not bother him? 'There must be other hotels . . .' she said. The silence had dragged painfully. Was Gideon waiting for her to speak?

He looked grim. 'There are—in the township, but I'd not let a girl of nineteen stay there alone.' Her checks were warm. 'I'm not a child.'

'No,' he said drily, 'but you happen to be a woman.' The little lame Cornishman spoke gently: 'The Contessa, sir?'

Gideon stared at the pointed elf-like face and the guileless blue eyes and smiled. 'Thanks for the suggestion, Pen. I get the message. But I'm afraid it won't work. The Contessa wouldn't like a guest—you know how hard it is to get her to come to dine.'

' 'Tain't right, sir, that's what I say,' Pen volunteered.

Gideon sighed. 'Don't we all, Pen? Where does it get us? We try . . .'

Mia wondered who the Contessa was and why she was so obviously anti-social. Perhaps she was some embittered old woman. Mia wondered at the sincere regret in Gideon's voice. The more of this man that she knew, the more he surprised her. One moment, she thought, she was hating him madly for his arrogance—the next, she was amazed by the compassion he could show. It didn't make sense.

Gideon got into the carriage, looking with unfriendly eyes at Mia. 'There's only one solution, I'm afraid. You'll have to come to my home.' He looked up at Pen, who hastily grinned and as hastily coughed in an attempt to hide it. 'Home, Pen.'

Mia tried to stand up, but Gideon pushed her back into the seat. 'I'm not going to impose on you,' Mia said stiffly.

He smiled. 'You have no choice.'

'But—but I can't,' Mia said unhappily. She turned to look at him. 'Mr. Eastwood, you were good enough to fly me out here, but I can't . . .'

'Are you afraid of me?' he asked, his voice cold, and then there was a gleam of amusement in his grey eyes. 'Don't worry, you'll have a very able chaperone—my grandmother.'

'It—it wasn't that . . .' Mia stopped, hesitating.

She did not dare to speak, for tears were near and she could imagine how scathing Gideon would be if she wept, but she wanted to curl up in a corner and hide, to howl like a disappointed child. Everything had gone wrong. Why must she always be at fault where Gideon was concerned? Why hadn't she thought to check back at the travel bureau? It had never entered her head, but to be dumped on an island like this, with nowhere to live, and her only choice was to be an even greater nuisance to this man who obviously disliked as well as despised her.

'I'm sorry—sorry I'm being such a nuisance to you,' she said humbly.

Gideon stared, puzzled, and then smiled. 'My dear silly child, you've got the wrong end of the stick. You won't be a nuisance. My grandmother will be thrilled to have you visit us, and didn't you see the big grin Pen tried to hide? Pen knows very well that it'll mean driving you round the island—which he'll love doing—also having someone new to talk to.'

Mia looked at Gideon worriedly. 'You're sure?' she asked uncertainly. 'It's very good of you.'

Gideon sighed, his mood changing with the speed of a jet plane. 'Oh, for crying out loud,' he said impatiently, 'do I have to dot every "i" and cross every "t", girl? Continual thanks can become a bore.'

He paused, a scowl spoiling his usual good looks. There was a strange glitter in his eyes that disturbed Mia. She never quite knew where she was with Gideon—was he really angry or just teasing? she wondered. This seemed a lot of anger over a very small thing. After all, if she wasn't grateful, he'd be the first to moan about it, she thought, the anger stirring inside her, helping her fight her distress at having to be more obliged to him.

'Look, Mia,' Gideon began again, his voice calm. 'Let's face it, shall we? You don't like me. You've made that very obvious, and here we are, landed with one another. I'm making the best of it, so you might as well do the same. We'll just keep out of one another's way. No fireworks in front of my grandmother, is that plainly understood? She's eighty-odd and hates angry disturbances, so we'll control our private feelings when we're with her, see? I've got a lot of work to do here—of course I don't know what you plan to do, but we can manage to avoid one another.'

He leaned forward, his voice changing again as he said curtly to Pen: 'Your horse is getting lazy. Time he tasted a touch of the whip.'

'What you say goes, sir,' Pen replied, whirling the long whip round his head and cracking it noisily.

Mia caught her breath with dismay. Horrified, she waited for the poor horse to jump under the pain of the stinging blow . . . and then she saw that the whip had hit the bough of the tree they were passing under and that the horse had not even noticed it, for he was jogging along at his leisurely contented pace.

Gideon laughed. Startled, Mia turned to stare at him. He stopped laughing, but there was still this strange look in his eyes.

'What's the joke?' she asked stiffly.

'Your face!' Gideon said, and began to

laugh again. He stopped abruptly, his voice changing. 'Honestly, Mia,' he said, sounding exasperated, 'it amazes me—you always expect the worst of me, don't you?'

She had no need to reply. She knew that her red cheeks had already spoken for her.

They jogged along in silence while Mia wondered if she should apologise but then decided it could only complicate things still more. She looked round her, trying to take in the incredible beauty of everything and so forget Gideon.

But it was hard to forget him, for every time the carriage jolted over the uneven road, she was swung against him, and each time she touched him a tiny shiver went through her. What a strange place this island was, she thought, a mass of contradictions. Just like Gideon, she added to herself.

Now they were ambling down what could be an English lane, she thought, the trees meeting overhead, shutting out the heat, and coming to a pair of wrought-iron gates that belonged to an English manor, surely. The horse seemed to recognise his home, for he lifted his head and began to trot down the winding drive, past great plants of vivid coloured flowers—deepest blue, scarlet, golden yellow, deep white. Mia's head began to ache with the beauty of it all and she suddenly wondered what Gideon's grandmother would be like. Would she be moody, difficult and as impossible as Gideon?

Mia wondered, suddenly nervous.

Gideon helped her out of the carriage, silent, his face strained as if he was still angry about something. The house was L-shaped, facing the ocean, protected from the winds by the mountain behind it. Here the palm trees were straighter than any she had seen on the rest of the island, she was thinking, as the dark green door opened and a dark-skinned butler stood there, his teeth flashing as he greeted Gideon and his eyes bright with surprised curiosity, as he looked at Mia.

As they stepped over the very English doormat, Gideon's face changed. He smiled, turned to Mia and said lightly :

'First, we must introduce you to my grandmother.'

He hurried her through the hall, which gave her only time to get a vague impression of polished black and white tiles, of portraits of stern-looking admirals and beautiful, elegant wives with off-the-shoulder gowns and strings of pearls and elaborately done hair—and then they went through a room where the deep blue carpet seemed to welcome her feet almost too lovingly as her shoes sank into the pile. Here she got a vague impression of shining walnut furniture, of glistening silver, bright glass, and then they walked through open French windows on to a wide terrace.

A little old woman sitting in a wheelchair turned to stare at them. She looked frail, Mia first thought, but then Mia saw the serenity of her face, the happiness in her blue eyes, the sweetness of her smile.

'Gideon, *mon petit choux!*' she said happily, and then her eyes passed on to Mia, and Mia saw the amazement—as there had been in the butler's eyes—immediately replaced by pleasure. 'My dear child—welcome to our lovely island,' the old lady said, holding out her hand in welcome.

Mia took the hand, bent and kissed it, startled by her action yet knowing instinctively that this was the only way to greet such a distinguished, unique person.

'Grand'mère,' Gideon said, 'I'd like to introduce Mia. She's on—on holiday here and I flew her out as there was no other means of transport at the moment. She booked in at the guest house, but it's closed.'

The old lady nodded. 'Reg was ill and Phoebe had to take him to Victoria for an operation.'

'So I've asked Mia to stay with us until something else can be arranged—if that's all right?'

The old lady laughed. 'Don't tease, you bad boy, you know that it is more than all right with me.' She smiled at Mia. 'Mia . . . Mia,' the old lady repeated. 'What a charming name. I could weep with joy, my child, at the sight of you. It is too long—far too long since I talked to so young a girl.'

Gideon had brought forward a deep wicker chair for Mia to sit in and was now stretched out lazily on a wicker couch, his hands clasped under his head, his legs crossed. He turned to smile at his grandmother.

'Don't tease her about her youth, Grand'mère, she is very sensitive.'

Mia blushed. 'I'm not! It's just—'

The old lady laughed. 'Take no notice of that bad boy, Mia my child, he was always a tease.'

Madame le Bret, as Mia discovered was the old lady's name as they talked, told Mia about the beautiful stillness of the island. 'Here I can forget the world and its horrors,' Madame le Bret said. 'I live in Paradise.'

'A cowardly retreat from reality,' Gideon said with a grin.

The old lady turned at once. 'And why should I not make such a retreat, *mon petit choux?* You love the battle of life, the fighting, the problems, the conflicts. I hate them. I love peace, good friends, harmony. With you, it is the same?' and she turned to look at Mia enquiringly.

I—' Mia hesitated. 'I don't know,' she said honestly. 'I lived in a small English village where my father was vicar, so somehow I was always involved in local feuds and quarrels. Sometimes I hated it—they seemed so petty.'

'You loved it. You're not bad at fighting yourself, Mia,' Gideon drawled, his eyes amused. 'You spare no punches,' he said, and began to laugh.

'Gideon,' Madame le Bret said sternly, 'this child must be tired after such a long flight. It is not proper to tease her until her strength is regained.' She smiled at Mia. 'I am on your side, Mia, one hundred per cent.'

'Thank you,' said Mia, 'I need an ally badly.' She flashed a triumphant look at Gideon and saw that he was staring at her oddly—in that same intense way that had attracted her notice and disturbed her composure on that first meeting, as she waited by Ian's side to be introduced to his friends as his fiancée.

Madame le Bret obviously noticed it too, for she leaned forward and tapped Gideon sharply with her small fan. 'Attention, Gideon,' she said sharply. 'Your manners. It is not polite to stare so at a young lady.'

Gideon sat up abruptly. 'Am I? I'm sorry, Mia.' He smiled at her. 'It's a failing of mine, as Mia knows. I can never stop staring at her.'

'You must succeed, Gideon,' Madame le Bret said. 'It is not comfortable nor pleasant for a girl to have a man stare at her in such a way.'

'I apologise humbly,' said Gideon, with laughter in his eyes, 'it's something about her face that . . .'

'Fascinates you?' Madame le Bret suggested. Gideon hesitated. 'No, let's say disturbs me.'

'Is my face so strange?' Mia asked stiffly.

The old lady nodded approvingly. 'Very good, my child. Stand up to this arrogant spoiled man who thinks he is so superior to us!'

Gideon looked embarrassed, something Mia had never expected to see. 'I don't, Grand'mère, honestly I—'

His grandmother laughed gaily. 'You act as if you do!'

Gideon laughed too. 'I bit that.' He turned to Mia. 'I must warn you, be on guard, for she's a great tease.'

'To return to the matter under discussion, Gideon,' said Madame le Bret, 'what is it about Mia that makes you stare? She is a very lovely girl, I know, but you have met millions of lovely girls and not stared at them.' A smile played round her mouth. 'Is it the combination of her fair hair and surprisingly green eyes? Is it her high cheekbones—how an artist would love to paint your face, my child, and probably break his heart because he would fail to catch that ethereal look.'

Mia fidgeted uncomfortably, her cheeks suddenly hot.

Gideon smiled. 'No, let us admit that Mia has good looks, if you like that kind of very young, very innocent look . . . but it's not that. I don't know what it is, but my eyes are drawn again and again to her face and so I'm called rude! Maybe she reminds me of someone.'

Mia's heart seemed to skip a beat. Was that a clue, she wondered, a clue to the discovery of her mother? If Gideon frequently came to this island, then he probably knew her real mother. Maybe she was like her mother, Mia thought. Perhaps that was the clue that would guide her. Now she must search among the women on the island who looked like her, she thought, new hope springing up inside her.

Later she was taken to her bedroom, a beautiful lofty room lavishly furnished and with her own bathroom, and a view of the lagoon. Everything was good, she thought, and felt the springs of the bed which were marvellous—but it was a different form of wealth from that of the Yates, her future parents-in-law.

The thought brought her to a standstill. She opened her French window and went outside, the warm air welcoming her, the beauty before her delighting her, but her heart was suddenly heavy. She had forgotten all about poor Ian since she left him.

If only, she thought, she'd had the courage to tell him the truth before she left—that she no longer wanted to marry him. But was it the truth? She had loved Ian very much—maybe she could love him again, if only she could make him see how impossible it was for her to live the sort of life his parents expected of her. Perhaps they could find a solution, if he loved her as much as he said he did, perhaps they could compromise.

She showered, thinking of what Madame le Bret had told her and marvelling at the beauty and elegance of the old lady. She had a French maid who did her snow-white hair in its elaborate style, her clothes were designed for her of soft pastel shades and incredible elegance, her every movement was graceful, her smile so beautiful . . .

Making up her face very carefully, Mia wondered, though, how anyone of Madame's intelligence and love of her fellow-creatures could have, as Madame le Bret had told Mia, lived on this island for over thirty years.

'Why should I leave when everything I love is here—even my memories of my beloved husband who died twenty years ago—of my beautiful daughter who married George Eastwood and was killed in an accident with him when Gideon was a small boy. Here I have memories. In another land, I would be completely alone,' Madame le Bret had said.

Dressing swiftly and choosing a buttercup yellow frock, Mia wished her father could have been with her on this island. How he would have loved the peaceful beauty—how well he and Madame le Bret would have got on, for both shared the same philosophy, ethics, and belief in the innate goodness of mankind. No wonder Gideon had got on well with her father—Gideon would have seen much of his grandmother in the vicar of Hawbridge.

Each day that passed was perfect—hours spent with Pen as he drove them both round the island, Madame le Bret seeming to enjoy the outings. Pen proved to have more strength than Mia expected, for he would lift the little old lady from her wheelchair and comfortably put her in the carriage, arranging a cushion at her back, a light dust-rug over her knee. They obviously enjoyed one another's company. Pen looking as rapt and awed as if he was serving a queen.

Sometimes Madame le Bret took Mia to meet her friends.

'Later, when Gideon has gone, we will entertain,' she told Mia.

When he has gone, Mia repeated silently. Somehow she could not imagine the island without Gideon on it. Not that she saw much of him, for he was out all day, only appearing at meals.

Madame le Bret was always talking about him. 'Gideon's manner is his armour, his defence, how d'you say?—his is a dynamic personality—all women tingle when he touches their hands or even smiles at them. When he walks into a room, no one else exists. I know. Even I, an old woman, feel it.'

'I know,' Mia said, for it was true.

'He disturbs you also?' Madame la Bret

asked.

Mia laughed. 'Only his moods. It's like walking on a tightrope at times, wondering if you're going to say the wrong thing.'

Madame le Bret patted Mia's hand gently. 'I know, my child. His beautiful mother was like that, too.'

'Why does he need a defence?' Mia asked.

The old lady looked startled. 'You are not serious? You must surely know. Gideon is always chased by women. You—you are different, for you are naïve, romantic and very sweet. No such thought would enter your head. Gideon is a wealthy, handsome man, but I know that if he was but a fisherman, battling to earn a meagre living, it would be the same. It is something about him . . .'

His arrogance, Mia thought. His air being able to control everything and everyone. So many women fell for that, she told herself. She preferred kindness, compassion.

Madame le Bret was talking again. 'I often think he comes to this island to escape, but even here he is not safe. Tonight Gideon will dine with a very beautiful lady whom I love dearly, yet I am fearful for she would not be good for Gideon. How can I tell him that? He would laugh at me, call me an interfering old busybody.'

'Yet you like her?' Mia said, startled for a moment.

They were being driven along in the

carriage and Pen's pointed ears were alert, so Madame le Bret lowered her voice.

'She carries guilt. A burden of guilt. We have told her so often that it was not her fault, but she will not believe. Guilt is not good to live with, *ma chérie.* Nor is it good for the man she marries. He will be her whipping-boy.'

Mia wanted to laugh. Anyone suggesting that Gideon, tall, with his broad shoulders, square chin and arrogance, could be a 'whipping-boy' was just hilariously funny, she thought, but obviously Madame le Bret did not agree, for she touched Mia's hand tightly.

'Make no mistake, my child, Gideon is vulnerable. Maybe more so than you, for he is a man and men can be deeply hurt. Gideon was once jilted by a girl and he has never recovered.'

Mia turned so sharply that she saw she had startled Madame le Bret. 'Gideon—jilted?' she exclaimed. This she did not—could not believe!

Madame le Bret nodded. 'It was very sad. Gideon was twenty-two years old, a romantic in many ways. She was a model—world-famous and very beautiful. But the other man had more money than Gideon. He was also a very old man and doubtless she had to think of her future . . .' Madame le Bret gave a little shrug of her thin shoulders.

'It hurt Gideon badly to learn that she had loved him for his money alone. Never before had he thought of money as an asset. His pride was jolted severely. He is always on guard—and will not be caught so easily again.' She paused. 'I hope!'

Mia thought of Miss Vaughan. Was she in love with the man or with his money? she wondered. Remembering the look on Gwyneth Vaughan's face, she decided it was a mixture of both. She wondered what Madame le Bret thought of Gwyneth.

Every afternoon Madame le Bret took a siesta and Mia would swim in the warm lagoon and lie in the sun on the beach, half-asleep, her thoughts drifting. One afternoon she woke up, covered with sand and gorgeously drowsy, and strolled down the warm sand for a swim. It was heavenly to float idly in the water, feeling the gentle flow of it, looking up through half-closed eyes at the blue sky. She was beginning to understand Madame le Bret's reluctance to leave the island. Here everything was so quiet and beautiful, no news of fights or car accidents or starving people.

Retreat from reality, Gideon had called it, teasing the old lady, but in a way he was right.

She thought of how little she had seen of Gideon since they arrived, except at meal times. She knew he was avoiding her. Several time she had been reading on the terrace and had seen him look through one of the French windows and hastily withdraw. Obviously he thought it safer to avoid her, so that they could not lose their tempers and fight in front of his grandmother.

Or was he, Mia thought, as she slowly rolled over and began to swim ashore, afraid she might chase him?

She began to laugh, swallowed a mouthful of water and spluttered. She was still choking, half laughing, half coughing, as she walked up the warm white sand towards her towel. She had begun to dry herself when Gideon walked out from behind an avenue of palms, and she wondered how long he had been there.

'Enjoying yourself?' he asked.

Mia looked at him warily, the green towel draped round her, her matching eyes thoughtful. 'So much,' she said honestly. 'It's all so wonderful.'

'I go back to England in two days,' he said abruptly. 'D'you want a lift?'

Mia stared at the tall man in immaculately white shorts and shirt. His short, thick, dark hair was smooth, he had recently shaved. He looked so impeccably neat and clean, it wasn't true.

'Go back to England?' she echoed slowly, startled at the dismay that flooded her. She thought of England, waiting for a doubtful and delayed spring. She thought of Ian—of the Yates and her problem of telling them that she could not lead the sort of life they expected of Ian's wife.

But predominant among her thoughts was

the knowledge of what she had failed to do. She had forgotten to look for her real mother! The beauty and charm of the island and the lazily luxurious life had lulled her into thoughtlessness. The whole reason for her visit to the island had been forgotten . . . and she had been here nearly a week!

'Don't look so horrified,' Gideon said, sounding amused. 'I don't want you to go. Grand'mère would break her heart if you went so soon. But I was thinking,' he said slowly, some of the friendliness in his voice vanishing, 'of Ian.'

'Ian?' For a moment, Mia didn't understand, and then her cheeks burned. 'Oh, Ian! He'll understand. He expected me to stay several months anyhow, and I've written to him.'

'A letter isn't quite the same.'

Mia looked surprised. 'I don't think he'll really miss me, you know. He's working so hard at his job that I think I was more often a nuisance than anything else.'

'He's ambitious.' Gideon's voice had a flat note, but Mia felt herself tense. What cruel thing was he planning to say? Unthinkingly she dropped the towel, standing before him in her sea-green two-piece swimsuit, her chin lifted defiantly.

'Aren't you ambitious?' she asked.

There was a strange flicker in his eyes. 'Of course.'

'Then why imply that it's a crime for Ian to be ambitious?' she demanded.

He smiled, then sighed, a long-drawn-out melodramatic and maddening sigh. 'Honestly, Mia, I can't understand you. Your manners grow worse rather than better. I implied nothing. I merely asked a civil question and you jump down my throat.'

'It was the way you asked it.'

She was beginning to shiver. Why, why, she asked herself, does he always upset me like this? Why couldn't she just laugh it off and say lightly something like, 'Who isn't ambitious?'

Suddenly he stooped to pick up the towel, draping it round her, holding it a little longer than necessary, she thought, as she shivered again, but his face was grave.

'It's surprisingly easy to catch a chill here— the breeze is sometimes deceptive. Better run up to the house and change into a dress. You'd better rest, for the most beautiful lady on the island is dining with us tonight,' he said, and walked away.

Gathering her things, Mia obeyed him. She walked slowly up the warm sandy beach to the stone steps that led to the garden, and across the green velvet-like lawn. It was amazingly like an English garden with its neat lawn edges, the banks of flowers, the creepers over the stone house, yet it was completely different, for these were tropical plants, their colours overwhelmingly vivid, almost

96

intoxicatingly fragrant. Then she walked along the wide, shady terrace with its comfortable reclining chairs to her own bedroom.

As she showered and rubbed herself dry, she thought how beautiful the house was, with its high thatched roof and lofty large rooms that had been designed and furnished with a view to comfort—and not as a status symbol, or an effort to out-Jones the Joneses.

Madame le Bret's day was always full— Gideon brought her all the new books as they were published and she passed them on, after reading them, to the local library or hospital. Always there was music, soft but lovely, filling every corner of the house. Madame le Bret seemed to have an inexhaustible supply of records—something else Gideon brought on each visit. Gideon, the wonderful one, Mia thought resentfully.

She went to join the old lady on the terrace for tea, wearing a plain white dress with a deep red belt.

'I hear we're having a visitor for dinner,' Mia said as Madame le Bret wheeled herself out on to the terrace, her face flushed from her siesta but her eyes bright and alive.

'Yes, *ma chérie*,' the old lady, smoothing down her lilac-coloured silk frock, smiled at Mia. 'She is the one we talked of—the one who has locked herself away from the world because of her guilt. Poor soul. I must tell you the sad little story.'

'Is she the Contessa?' Mia asked, remembering Pen's suggestion when she arrived, and they had found the guest house was closed and there was no place for Mia to go; remembering also Gideon's implication that everyone had tried to help the Contessa without success.

'Yes, my child, the Contessa Annys Severini . . . I must warn you so that you do not show your shock. She is the most beautiful woman I have ever seen, but now it is as if a cloud has passed over her face, hiding the beauty. She has withdrawn from the world—she refuses to come back to it. It is so sad that we all wish at times to weep, for she is still young and oh, so very beautiful. Before the tragedy, she was always gay and loved to meet people.'

A soft-footed parlourmaid brought out the tea and, as she had grown used to doing, she poured it out into the eggshell-thin china, while she passed the delicate rolls of bread and butter and the exquisite rum babas to the old lady.

'What sort of tragedy was it?' Mia asked. She felt excited—eager to meet the Contessa, so she could see if she could possibly be her mother—yet her father had said her real mother was English. The name Annys was unusual and Severini was definitely Italian.

'Very, very sad,' said Madame le Bret, lightly wiping sticky fingers on her napkin. 'Her husband was a distinguished diplomat and they had been married ten years before they had a child, a delicate little girl. She was so small when she was born that no one thought she could live—but she did, and she was like a little doll. I saw her one year when they came to this island and bought the house in which Annys now lives. Then her husband was posted to another country and they went away. One day the Contessa was driving them home—I believe it was from church, but am not certain—and the car rolled over the edge of a mountainside.'

Madame le Bret paused and with one of her graceful gestures lightly wiped her eyes. 'It was not the Contessa's fault. Later it was proved that the steering had gone wrong, but she still blames herself. She was in hospital for nearly a year—both her husband and the little girl were killed.'

'How terrible!' Mia said softly, thinking to herself how very inadequate words were on such an occasion.

'It is terrible, but it should not mean the end of the world,' said Madame le Bret. 'Her husband would be sad at her unceasing sorrow. Nor should she blame herself for what was not her fault. We have tried—the little group of us who live on this side of the island. Next week, dear child, I am holding a series of dinner parties for my friends, but alas, they are all old folk. I am sad that there is no one of your age here.'

'Thanks be!' a deep familiar voice said as Gideon strode out on to the terrace. 'Can I have some tea, Mia?' he asked, helping himself to a rum baba. He looked at Madame le Bret. 'Have you been telling Mia about Annys?'

The old lady nodded. 'Yes, so that she will not be too shocked by her appearance.'

Gideon helped himself to sugar generously, Mia noticed. He was all solid muscle, she thought—lean, tough, almost overwhelmingly healthy.

'Poor Annys,' he said, and there was a gentleness in his voice that Mia had never heard before. 'I wish we could find a way to help her.'

'You do your best, my boy,' his grandmother said affectionately.

'And get nowhere . . . Shall I dress for dinner, Grand'mère darling?'

She pretended to look shocked. 'But of course, mon *petit choux.* We cannot have a naked man!'

He went and kissed her gently. 'You naughty old woman, I asked for that, didn't I? All right, I'll get my own back.'

She patted his cheek. 'Of course we will dress up—that is all Annys has left, Mia. Her beautiful clothes.'

Mia was not sure what she had expected the Contessa to be like, but as she stood by Madame le Bret's wheelchair to welcome their guest, she understood why the old lady had warned her.

The Contessa was tall and slim—so slim that you felt a puff of wind could blow her over. Her silky hair was fair and swept back from her high forehead, but her skin was so thin it was almost transparent. She wore a yellow silk gown, the same colour as her hair. Her face was pale. She looked like the most beautiful ghost Mia had ever seen—as she came closer, Mia could see that her eyes had a distant look as if, as Madame le Bret had said, she had retreated from a world that could hold only pain for her.

'My dear child,' Madame le Bret said softly, 'it is a pleasure to have your company. This is Mia, my little friend.'

The Contessa looked at Mia, but Mia was sure she did not see her, except as a blur and a form who must be spoken to politely. Close behind the Contessa was Gideon, tall, broad-shouldered, protective as he helped the frail, beautiful zombie—for that was how the Contessa seemed to Mia, a robot. Gideon was wearing a white jacket and black trousers, a white silk shirt. He looked very handsome, she thought, watching the way he looked after the Contessa.

Glancing at Madame le Bret, Mia saw the concern on the old lady's face, and remembered that she had said that Gideon was in danger from the Contessa.

It was a strange meal, everyone talking

politely, the conversation never dying, and yet there was an atmosphere of whispering, and yet they did not whisper. Mia could not describe it, yet she felt they were all talking carefully, terrified of saying the wrong thing, of hurting this beautiful woman who smiled and spoke but just was not there.

After the dinner, they sat on the terrace, flaming torches burning to keep away the mosquitoes and moths. They had coffee and liqueurs and a beautifully cool breeze blew in from the ocean.

'You like it here?' the Contessa asked Mia.

'I think it's very beautiful, and so . . . so peaceful,' Mia told her.

A smile curved the beautiful line of the Contessa's mouth. 'But at your age, it is not peace you seek, surely?' The Contessa had no accent, she could have been English, Mia thought, yet she had a rather formal, almost pedantic way of speaking at times.

'At the moment, yes,' Mia told her.

Gideon leaned forward to interrupt, in case, Mia thought, the Contessa asked her why and Mia mentioned the obviously forbidden word 'death'. 'What did you think of the town, Mia? I hear Pen took you over there,' Gideon asked.

'I found it fascinating, such a mixture of people,' Mia turned to him, grateful for the interruption. 'The painted houses, the surprisingly modern church, the fishing village, the yachts. It was all so different from this part of the island. It seemed quite odd to see trains and cars . . . How d'you keep them away from here?'

Gideon laughed. 'We charge a toll fee for visitors coming over and they have to travel by carriage. Ask Pen to show you the tourists' centre as we call it,' he chuckled. 'We're pretty arbitrary, I know, but we don't want to spoil this part and it's all private property.'

'I can understand.'

Later, after the Contessa had risen, thanked her hostess gracefully and departed, Gideon going out to see her into her carriage, Madame le Bret looked at Mia. 'Well?'

'She's very beautiful, but . . .'

Madame le Bret lifted her finger. 'But . . . ? How well you have it summed up, my child. But . . . She does not live, that poor soul.'

'She certainly wasn't with us.'

Gideon returned to join them and his grandmother smiled. 'She asked Mia a question, Gideon. That was progress, I think.'

'Definitely,' he said gravely. 'She also asked me questions about her. I think she likes you, Mia.' His voice was thoughtful as he looked at her. 'And you?'

'I was a little scared—of saying the wrong thing,' Mia confessed.

He nodded, 'I know. There is an aura of— not fear, perhaps it's anxiety. It's so easy to say the wrong thing, and then she cries and we have to send for the doctor. It is something beyond her control, he says. She feels there is nothing left in life to live for.'

'That's absurd,' said Madame le Bret.

She looked at the beautiful diamond-studded fob watch pinned on her elegant bluebell-mauve frock. 'It is time I slept, I think.' She tinkled a little bell and the heavily-jowled butler came to her side. 'Wait, Jacob, a moment. Gideon, have you shown Mia the waterfall by moonlight? You have not? Then tonight with the full moon is a perfect time.'

Gideon rose. 'Of course, Grand'mère.' He waited until the big butler with his dark face and spotless clothes wheeled the old lady out of sight, and then Gideon turned to Mia. 'Care to see it? It's quite something.'

'I'd love to,' said Mia, lulled by his friendliness. She had chosen her dress carefully, had seen the look of approval in Madame le Bret's eyes; now she wondered what Gideon thought as she stood up, for he was staring at her strangely. It was a green dress, high-waisted, with a little velvet band round the waist tied into a neat bow. Round the hem of the full skirt—it was made of a special kind of silk and hung in soft folds—was a matching green velvet band. Her shoulders were bare and she had put on a simple chain of white shells she had bought on the island, thinking that her sun-browned skin made the white shells glow.

Gideon grinned at her. 'Not bad—the dress,

I mean.'

'Thanks,' smiled Mia. 'I thought the Contessa's dress was lovely.'

Gideon's hand was under her elbow as he helped her down the steps to the lawn. She shivered for a moment. 'Chilly?' he asked, but when she looked at him, she saw the amusement in his eyes, and her cheeks burned, for she knew he had recognised the reason for her shiver.

She wished she had not said she would walk with him in the moonlight. But now it was too late. It would only evoke sarcastic remarks, a teasing she did not feel in the mood to take good-temperedly.

'Yes,' he went on, 'Annys's gown was very beautiful. It probably cost twenty times what yours cost—her husband was a very wealthy man.'

'It must be terrible for her,' Mia said as they walked across the smooth lawn, and she saw the wide silver streak of moonlight across the lagoon. It was quiet, so very quiet and beautiful. The deep shadows the palm trees cast over the lawn, the soft lap-lap of the water, and from the house they were leaving behind came the strains of soft music. 'I mean, to have been driving the car when . . .'

Gideon helped her cross a small rustic bridge. Far below was a tiny stream meandering over white pebbles. 'Yes, but the accident could have happened to anyone,'

Gideon said, 'not that I would ever trust a woman driver.'

'But that's absurd, there are good and bad drivers of both sex,' Mia said quickly. 'You know—you know, you're so biased, it's almost farcical!'

'Farcical?' he repeated, and he sounded amused.

'Yes, you're so biased against women that it sounds as if you're scared of them.' The darkness gave her courage.

'I'm not scared of women,' he said, putting emphasis on the last word.

'Then why d'you despise us, why can't you see us as equals?'

He laughed, throwing back his head to do so. 'Now you're being farcical, my dear girl. How could man and woman be equal? We're each perfect in our own sphere . . . Look out,' he said sharply, but just too late, for Mia had not seen the tree root and had tripped. She would have fallen headlong, but Gideon caught her, helped her stand up, brushed his hand on her dress. 'I hope you didn't tear it.'

She was breathless for a moment. It was, of course, from the shock of falling, she told herself. Suddenly she heard a strangely beautiful sound, a kind of singing.

'That's the stream,' Gideon said. As if both had forgotten the foolish quarrel they had started, he led her to a wide opening. They were standing just below a tall outcrop of rock;

106

it had a strange shape as if it had been modelled by a skilful but giant hand. Down the rock tumbled the stream, falling into a pool, causing tiny whirlpools so that the white lilies rocked on their green leaves. The moonlight turned the stream of water into silver.

'It's lovely!' Mia said softly.

Gideon spread a handkerchief on the rock. 'Shall we sit down?' he asked. He offered her a cigarette and lit it and then lit one for himself. They sat in silence, the deep stillness seemed to envelop Mia like a comforting blanket.

She turned impulsively to the man by her side. 'Gideon, I'd have thought this lovely place would have helped the Contessa?'

He studied the glowing tip of his cigarette. 'I think it could if she would let it, Mia. The trouble is that she won't face up to the truth— that she has lost the man she loved and the child she idolised. I knew her husband well. Until the child was born, Annys was restless, brittle with gaiety, if you know what I mean. Always seeking something. The child gave her that something. But she lost it. Even more terrible to Annys is the fact that she feels it was her hand that destroyed the child.'

He flicked the ash off his cigarette and turned to look at Mia. 'You can't run away from the truth, Mia. It's no good trying to escape by refusing to admit it. Yet that's what you're doing, isn't it?'

She was startled. 'Me?'

He nodded. 'You can't make up your mind about Ian, can you? One moment you love him—the next moment you're not sure. Have you thought how unfair this is to Ian? He trusts you. Aren't you dragging out the agony for him by this long delay in making up your mind? Wouldn't it be much kinder to tell him frankly that you can't marry him?'

'But I'm not sure,' Mia said slowly.

Gideon stood up. 'Are you out of your mind?' he asked roughly. 'When you love anyone—really love them, that is—you know it. There never can be any shadow of doubt.'

They walked home in silence, Mia remembering the way Gideon had said: 'You know it.'

Did he love the Contessa? she wondered. His grand-mother feared he did. But could you love a beautiful woman who looks at you blankly and who speaks automatically, without warmth or life?

Yet if you love someone, really love them, Gideon had said, you know it.

CHAPTER FIVE

When Gideon came out to the terrace to say goodbye, Mia, playing chess with Gideon's grandmother, looked up.

As so often before, she thought that Gideon

was almost too perfect to be human. It would be easier to like him if he had more faults and seemed a normal person. Why had he to be so tall that he towered above everyone? So broad-shouldered that you felt his strength, even though he did not touch you?

Smiling down at his grandmother as he spoke gently to her, Gideon was wearing a tropical suit of pale grey. His grey silk tie, white silk shirt were perfect. Mia knew he had no valet, yet he looked as if a dozen valets had groomed him. His black shoes shone, his grey socks were a continuation of the grey of his suit.

He glanced at her. 'Don't want to change your mind, Mia?' he asked. 'There's room for you in the plane, you know.' His voice was teasing, almost mocking, as if he knew that the last thing in the world she wanted was to fly back to England and the problem that awaited her.

'Stop it, you naughty boy,' Madame le Bret scolded. 'Do not even hint at taking my dear Mia from me.' Even though she must have known he was teasing, she got excited and reverted to her favourite language. *'Jamais— jamais. Tout à fait impossible.* I do not wish for her to go . . .' And then the old lady turned to Mia, her face changing. 'He is teasing, no? You do not want to go—yet?'

There was something inexpressibly pathetic in that little word 'yet', and Mia saw that it went home to Gideon as well as to her, for even as she patted the thin, veined old hand and said of course she wasn't going, Gideon was apologising.

'A joke that misfired, Grand'mère,' he said. 'I was teasing. When Mia is ready to go, she will tell us in good time.'

He lifted his hand in farewell and walked out to where the carriage, the white horse, and Pen waited patiently, there to be carried at a gentle leisurely trot to the air-strip. Mia was thinking, and from there to be lifted into the sky by the plane's powerful engines and carried at the rate of hundreds of miles an hour and finally to London, with its roar of traffic that never softened, the scurrying people on the pavements, the buses that crawled, nose to tail. To a life so utterly different from this, Mia thought, as she watched him go.

Madame le Bret's eyes were anxious. 'You are happy here, Mia?'

Mia nodded. 'Very, very happy. Sometimes I think I'll never want to go away.'

Madame le Bret glanced significantly at Mia's engagement ring. 'He would not like that.'

Mia laughed. 'He would be lost here.' She told the old lady, who never asked questions, a little about Ian and his family. 'Ian changed so much,' she finished, her voice puzzled. 'Almost overnight.'

'And you are no longer sure,' said Madame le Bret, but it was not a question.

Mia sighed. 'No, I'm not sure.'

That night over dinner, Madame le Bret said sadly: 'This chilly stillness fills the house when my Gideon leaves. I am only grateful he comes when he can, but a small part of me dies each times he goes. Tomorrow we start to entertain,' she added, smiling with a brittle gaiety. 'Always I do this when my Gideon goes. I fill the house with my friends and so the cold quietness goes. I only wish, my dear child, that there were young people here for you to meet. Most of them are elderly or retired.'

'You don't get many young people here?' Mia asked, and then corrected herself: 'I don't mean very young, I mean in their late thirties.'

Madame le Bret chuckled. 'How can you tell the age of a woman who is beautiful? The Contessa? Her age—I would not know. Perhaps thirty, thirty-five, or maybe forty-five. Her eyes are so old with sorrow that it hides her age. When you meet Phoebe Haseldine, it is the same. She runs the guest house and is an unhappy woman, for she has an invalid husband who is jealous, possessive and cruel. Unintentionally, of course. Her face is young and so is her skin, but in her eyes is a look of failure. Without success, she struggles to make her husband happy. She is a dear friend of mine. You will love her, but when you say what is her age—what answer could I give? She might be thirty—which I doubt—forty perhaps. Who can tell? Last year we had a widow here. She was about their age, but as I say, it was impossible to tell. She was very unhappy and grieved, but she had courage and came here to overcome her sorrow. She was here three years, but then she left. She has, perhaps, met someone and is tasting happiness.'

'What was her name?' Mia asked eagerly. Maybe her real mother had only just left the island; if that was so, perhaps she could trace her. Annys, Phoebe and this unknown woman—here were three possibles . . .

Then Mia saw the surprise on Madame le Bret's face and wished she had not asked the question, for it was stupid. Why should she want to know the name of someone she had never met—nor was ever likely to meet, or so Madame le Bret would think.

But the old lady thought for a moment. 'Madeleine, I remember. A strange surname. Fox, perhaps. Phoebe would know, for they were close friends.' She rang the little silver bell. 'We will have our coffee here, if you do not mind, Mia. I am a little weary and would like to go to bed soon.'

'Of course,' Mia said at once, knowing it was not weariness the old lady was feeling but sadness because Gideon had gone.

Later, Mia walked to the edge of the sand. Great clouds swept across the sky, throwing strange shadows on the ground. She wished she could confide in Gideon's grandmother—it would be such a help.

Mia walked along the sand. How easy it would be to stay here indefinitely, to drift along, enjoying the beauty, the peace, the luxury, and postponing the finding of her mother. But how could she do this? First she must remember Ian, and her promise to marry him.

She found a rock, carved as if by Nature to fit her back, and sat there, hands clasped round her knees, eyes thoughtfully resting on the lagoon.

Ian! She had loved him, very much. That was one thing she knew for sure. They liked the same jokes, enjoyed being together. Wasn't that the best recipe for a happy marriage?

Supposing she went back to England and married Ian, Mia thought, could they find happiness together? She stifled a sigh—she was sure they could if they were left alone. But that was the crux of the matter—they wouldn't be left to lead their lives alone. They would have to do what Ian's parents, the Yates, told them to do. And that was what she feared.

She walked back to the house, as far removed from her decision as when she walked out of it. That night she slept fitfully and woke up, feeling absurdly sad, and then she remembered: Gideon had gone back to London and she was left with two—it seemed, unsolvable—problems.

One late afternoon Pen was driving Mia home from a tea-party, and as they passed through the gates he saw a plump brown pony grazing. Pen turned to look down at Mia.

'Mrs. Haseldine, she's here. That pony there, he belongs to her. You wouldn't be leaving us, be 'ee, Miss Mia?' he asked, and sounded anxious.

'I—I honestly don't know,' Mia told him.

Somehow she had forgotten the Haseldines and the guest house. What was it Gideon had said? She tried to remember. Was it that she should stay with them until the guest house re-opened?

'I don't know,' she repeated dully. 'I mean, I did book in there and Madame le Bret has been very good to me, but—'

'Eh, Miss Mia, but you be good for her.'

'I don't want to go,' she admitted.

But as she went into the house, she forgot her fears as she realised something—Phoebe Haseldine was here, and it was just possible Phoebe might be her real mother. Mia stood still in the hall, catching her breath, trying to gain courage.

Mia's steps were slow as she went to the terrace. One half of her was eager to see Phoebe—the other half was scared. She heard Madame le Bret's silvery laugh and a deep warm voice. Madame le Bret saw Mia and called :

114

'Come, my child, I want you to meet my dear friend.'

Mia walked outside tensely, her eyes fixed on the woman who stood up. Phoebe was tall, with long slender legs and small bones. So was she, Mia thought quickly. Phoebe's face was round, the cheekbones undistinguishable, her eyes blue. But her hair was honey brown. Mia could see no resemblance in Phoebe's face to her own—but then, she told herself, perhaps she took after her unknown father.

'I owe you an apology, Miss—' Phoebe began.

'Phoebe, she's Mia,' the old lady scolded gently.

Phoebe shook hands with Mia and smiled. 'Mia. What an unusual name! I hear I landed you in a very awkward situation, Mia. You see, I did get the cable booking you in, but at the time my husband was taken ill and I clean forgot. It was only yesterday when I got back and began tidying up that I found the cable. I'm so glad Gideon was on hand to help.'

'I'm so glad you lost the cable, Phoebe,' Madame le Bret said with a laugh. 'You cannot take Mia from me now.' Her frail hand closed over Mia's. 'You won't go, my child?'

Mia hesitated. 'But Gideon—'

Madame le Bret frowned. 'What has my mischievous grandson to do with it? Did he imply you would be a nuisance?'

Mia flushed. 'Oh, no. I was the one who said

that. He said I'd be company for you.'

The old lady nodded. 'As usual he was right. Please stay, Mia.'

Mia laid the old hand against her cheek for a moment. 'There's nothing I'd like more, Madame le Bret. I'm happy here, so very happy.'

Later, she and Phoebe walked along the sand, talking. Tentatively Mia asked questions, but she learned very little.

'Have I lived here long?' Phoebe asked with a smile. 'Sometimes it seems like my whole life. No, we have no children—unfortunately. My husband never wanted them, I think he feared he'd lose me. Some men do, you know, Mia. I've been told it's a mistake to devote yourself too much to your children.'

'But your child needs you,' Mia blurted out, and then wished she hadn't.

Phoebe looked at her. 'I have known children who were better off for being looked after by someone else, Mia. A mother can become too involved emotionally, and that may harm the child. My mother was like that. She had to possess me. She had to choose the man I was to marry, I had to live where she thought best, wear the clothes she chose . . .'

'It sounds just like Ian's parents,' said Mia, and told Phoebe about Ian and the Yates, the way Ian had changed. 'He's a different man— and I'm not sure if I like this new man,' she confessed, surprised that she could talk so easily and so soon to Phoebe.

It was as if Phoebe felt the same. 'My husband was a world-famous athlete until he was hurt in a car crash. Now he's a permanent invalid, he needs me all the time. If I had children, a boy to worry about or a girl to try to communicate with, how could I look after him? Usually, Mia, you'll find that things work out for the best, though you don't think so at the time.'

That evening, over chess, the old lady talked about Phoebe.

'Gideon and I are very fond of them, though at times Gideon is impatient with Reg. Gideon is so strong, so sure of himself, that he can be intolerant of weakness,' she admitted. 'He feels Reg is unfair to Phoebe. She is Reg's whipping-boy, he has to have revenge on fate for the way he has been treated, so he makes poor Phoebe suffer.'

Mia nodded; it was odd, but 'whipping-boy' was a favourite expression of Madame le Bret's. She had said the Contessa would use her next husband as one.

'Do we all have whipping-boys, Madame le Bret?' she asked.

The old lady smiled and touched Mia's cheek gently. 'I'm afraid so, dear.'

'But Ian can't be my whipping-boy,' Mia said, thinking aloud. 'I mean, I felt like this before Daddy died.'

'No, Mia,' the old lady said gently, 'Ian is

117

not your whipping-boy, dear child. I'm afraid it is Gideon.'

She stared at the sympathetic aged face, at the gallantly-elegant hair, the loving blue eyes, and she searched her mind. Was Madame le Bret right? she asked herself.

Looking back, she remembered how quickly she had thought the worst of Gideon when he ordered Pen to whip the old horse. Perhaps Gideon understood—because he had laughed and said she always expected the worst of him. Did she? Was that why she got so bad-tempered when everyone praised him? Why she disliked his air of cleanliness and power.

Was it—she thought, with sudden clarity—because Gideon had all the virtues Ian lacked and that she wished he had? Yet Gideon could be cruel. Maybe the things he had said of Ian were true, but had truth always to be cruel?

Could it be the reason for her hatred of Gideon? Because he had forced her to recognise the truth about Ian? Because he had made her realise that she could never, under any circumstances, marry Ian?

She stood up. 'Will you forgive me if I go to bed?' she asked the silent old lady.

'Of course, child,' Madame le Bret said gently. 'Sleep well and your problem will solve itself.'

*   *   *

118

The next day she wrote to Ian. It was easier than she had expected. She simply told him the truth.

First that she had loved him very much and was still fond of him, but that his mother was right, she felt she was too young to act the part that Ian's wife should act.

'I'm not good at entertaining people I dislike,' Mia wrote. 'I'm sorry, Ian, very sorry, but it's better for me to find out now than later. I hope you find the right kind of girl who can help you with your career just as your mother has helped your father.'

It was then that she thought of the best reason of all.

'Ian, this must be a secret between us, but I feel you should know. I came out here to look for my real mother. I didn't know until the day my "father" died that I was adopted. I had one clue that led to the island, but I can find no one here who could be my mother, at all. I shall go on trying, of course, but I know how much it means to your father to have good blood in the family. That's why my "father" told me the truth. He said it would be a terrible thing for us both if one day the truth was learned and your father might think I had deliberately deceived him. Please tell no one, as I shall always think of my adoptive parents as my real parents, for they were so good to me. Please try to understand and forgive.'

She packed her engagement ring carefully

and Pen drove her to the post office. Afterwards he drove her to the guest house to have tea with Phoebe.

'Don't wait, Pen,' Phoebe said. 'I'll drive Miss Mia home. Do my old Robin good to do a bit of work.'

Pen lifted his whip in salute and Nero ambled off contentedly.

Mia found it hard to like Phoebe's husband, Reg. A thin bald discontented man, he was unfriendly but not rude. His restless dark eyes followed every movement Phoebe made; if she was out of his room more than ten minutes he rang a small bell incessantly.

Someone—it was not Mia—started a discussion on adoption, and Reg expressed his view very decidedly.

'I could never accept or trust another man's child. I'd always be watching to see something bad in him, something he might have inherited. I'd not be like that with a child of my own blood. In any case, I'd be too jealous. Tell little Mia what a beast I am, Phoebe, never allowing you to go out alone, always doubting you.'

Phoebe went red. 'You're not a beast, Reg.'

Mia began to understand why, as Madame le Bret had told her once, Phoebe's friends rarely visited her. Later, alone with Phoebe, Mia was told to take no notice.

'Poor Reg can't help it,' Phoebe said. 'You see, we were both in the car and he was the only one injured. It was rather unfair, wasn't it?'

'He . . . he spoke very strongly about adopting children,' said Mia, a little nervous because each time she saw Phoebe, she felt more certain that Phoebe was her real mother. 'Suppose you'd been a widow with several children.'

'He'd never have married me,' Phoebe said simply. Phoebe drove her home, Robin, the fat old pony, wheezing for sympathy as he dawdled along.

'Take no notice,' Phoebe said to Mia, 'it's all an act. You should see him gallop round the paddock in the early morning. He's like all men—plays on our sympathy.' Her face changed. 'Except Gideon.' Her voice softened. 'We owe everything to Gideon, you know, Mia. He lets us have the guest house at a ridiculously low rent . . .'

Mia was not listening properly, for she was trying to digest the unpalatable truth that her visit had revealed. Reg's dislike and even hatred of another man's child. Suppose Phoebe was her mother, Mia was thinking, how would Reg react to the news? Perhaps Phoebe had never told him of that first elopement, the first baby that had to be adopted. How would Reg behave? If he was so jealous and possessive . . . Mia was beginning to understand now why her father—her adoptive father—had warned her to be careful.

Yet it was terribly tempting to tell Phoebe everything, to ask if it was the truth. Surely they could keep it a secret from Reg? Yet how could she say to Phoebe whom she had only recently met: 'Did you elope and have a baby at seventeen—if so, here I am!' It just couldn't be done, Mia told herself.

A plane zoomed overhead and Phoebe looked up.

'It can't be Gideon again so soon. . . he never comes as often.'

'We're not expecting him,' said Mia.

'Then he's probably sent out one of his staff. Sometimes his secretary comes.'

They drove through the English-looking wrought iron gates. 'You'll come in?' invited Mia.

Phoebe hesitated. 'I think not, Mia. If Reg has heard the plane and I'm up here a long time . . .' she smiled ruefully. 'Reg is grateful for what Gideon has done, but he still distrusts him where I'm concerned. Isn't it comic?'

Mia went straight to her room, showered because of the sticky heat and put on a clean dress just as a gentle knock came on the door. It was Madame le Bret's little French maid, looking scared.

'It's Monsieur,' she began.

So it was Gideon in the plane, Mia thought. Why had he come back so quickly? Was Madame le Bret ill—had the doctor secretly cabled him?

'Monsieur says to come to speak with him at once,' the little French maid said, her dark eyes wide. 'He says *vite* . . . 'urry . . . 'urry . . . he's . . .'

'Angry?' Mia asked. The girl nodded and turned and fled.

Slowly Mia walked to the study. Was it bad news about the old lady? she wondered, and she hurried suddenly. It must be urgent if he said so.

Fear made her open the study door even as she knocked, and when Gideon looked up from his desk, she knew that it had nothing to do with his grandmother—it was with herself that he was angry.

'Mia, why did you lie to me?' he asked harshly.

She thought she had never seen him so angry. He was still wearing the dark suit he must have worn in London, he looked tired, but his mouth was a thin line of fury.

'I—lie to you?' she said, her knees feeling suddenly weak, so she put out her hands to lean on the desk. 'What about?'

'Good grief,' he said wearily, 'must I spell everything out? Why didn't you tell me you had told Ian you were coming out to this island to visit some old friends of your father?'

Involuntarily Mia's hand flew in dismay to her mouth. Her eyes were wide with dismay. She had forgotten!

'I'm sorry. I—'

He gave her no chance to explain. 'Can you imagine the situation I found myself in?' he demanded. 'Ian came to see me. He was worried about you, he wanted to know if you were well and happy. He said your letters were unsatisfactory—were not like you. He didn't think it was due to grief for your father, he said he knew you better than that. He thinks you're trying to hide something from him. He wanted to know the kind of people you were staying with. Ian was—he was concerned about you, Mia.'

He paused and leaned forward. 'I was put in a very embarrassing situation. Was I to tell him the truth? That you had come out here—had so-say booked in at a guest house—and that you were living with my grandmother? In addition, I remembered your evasive replies when I asked a simple question—the reason you wanted to come to the island. What are you trying to hide, Mia?'

Somehow she found her voice. 'What did you tell Ian?'

'The truth. That you were well and happy. That you were staying with nice people and that he had no need to worry.'

'Thank you,' she said meekly. 'I'm sorry, I really am, Gideon. You see. . . you see, Ian didn't want me to come out here, he suggested somewhere nearer, and I had to tell him something.'

'You won't tell me why you came out?'

She shook her head. 'I—I can't.'

He frowned, ran his hand through his hair. 'I don't understand you, Mia. What is the big secret? Did your father want you to come out? How did you even hear of this place?'

'He told me about it.'

'He wanted you to come out?'

'In—in a way—but not at once. He wanted me to wait.'

'And why didn't you?'

'Because I couldn't bear to wait,' her voice rose a little. Whatever happened, she must keep her promise. Suddenly she knew what to say. 'I promised my father I wouldn't tell anyone.'

Gideon stared at her and burst out laughing. 'A likely story! How old d'you think I am, Mia? All right, if you won't tell me, short of torture, I don't suppose I can make you. Just one thing.' His face was stern. 'You're not employed by a travel agency, are you? I mean, they're not planning to start a holiday camp on this island, are they?'

He laughed at her puzzled look. Mia was so grateful that he had stopped cross-examining her that she felt dazed.

'I really am sorry, Gideon, about—about that. I quite forgot what I'd said to Ian.'

Gideon stood up. 'I think you'd better write him a nice letter and ease his fears.' He looked down at her hands; she was still leaning on the desk. 'Where's your ring? Lost it? Or have you come to your senses and broken off the engagement?'

Perhaps if she had not felt flustered by his questions, perhaps if he had spoken in a nicer way—if he had not sounded so amused and arrogant, Mia might have told him the truth. As it was, she suddenly knew that she could not bear to se his mocking triumphant smile.

'The ring keeps falling off when I'm swimming, so I've put it away safely,' she lied.

This time he believed her. 'Good idea, must have cost a lot.' He turned away. 'I'm busy, Mia, if you don't mind,' he dismissed her curtly. 'See you at dinner,' he said, sitting down, beginning to write, just as if she was not there.

He waited until she had her hand on the door. 'Mia, I wish you could trust me,' he said.

She took a long time to reply as she studied his face with its aquiline nose, shrewd cold grey eyes, and mouth that could be so relentlessly hard.

'I wish I could,' she said with a little sigh, and left the room.

CHAPTER SIX

At dinner, Madame le Bret seemed to glow with happiness.

'Just think, dear child,' she said to Mia,

'Gideon has promised to take a holiday. He will stay with us one week, two weeks, maybe four weeks, Gideon?'

Gideon smiled. 'It depends, Grand'mère, on so many things. I hope, for four weeks.' He looked wryly at Mia. 'If you can stand my company.'

Madame le Bret chuckled. 'We know we shall not see as much of you as we would like, Gideon. I have never known you take a real holiday. You will be at the shipyard, on the telephone, writing letters. I trust,' her voice sobered, 'I would be so happy, Gideon, if you could be here when my children come.'

Mia looked bewildered. She had never heard of Madame le Bret's children. Gideon turned and saw her look of bewilderment.

'There's an orphanage on the mainland, and once a year my grandmother invites about thirty of these children for a week's holiday. We put up tents in the garden and they practically live in the lagoon.'

'They love it,' Madame le Bret said simply.

Gideon chuckled. 'One thing, Mia can help you, Grand'mère. She's a trained nursery school teacher, aren't you?'

For some reason unknown to herself, Mia coloured. Why had Gideon always to say 'nursery school teacher' in that contemptuous tone? Perhaps because he didn't realise how important pre-school training was for young children, especially where there was only one child in the family.

Madame le Bret's reaction was much more complimentary. 'Mia—and you have not told me! I am so happy to know that, for it is not always easy when the children come. You must talk to me about your training. I am interested in everything to do with young people.'

'That is so obvious,' Gideon said quietly.

Mia glanced at him sharply and then at his grandmother, but she did not seem to have heard. Turning again to look at the man sitting opposite her, Mia saw the amusement in his eyes, and once again she coloured, hating herself for her weakness in 'biting.'

Over coffee on the terrace, with the great torches flaming, the graceful crescent of the moon sending silvery specks of light on the dark water, the palm trees moving slightly as if they were a ballet of dancers against the star-bright sky, Gideon asked Mia if she still enjoyed life on the island.

'Not bored?' he asked.

Startled, she spoke the truth impulsively. 'Of course not. I love it. Sometimes I wonder how I'll ever leave it.'

He gave her an odd look. 'Don't get too fond of it,' he said, significantly glancing down at her left hand.

Again Mia's cheeks were warm. She must remember that no one knew the truth—that the letter to Ian had gone off, and his ring too. She had lied to Gideon about that.

'I won't,' she said. 'Don't worry,' she added.

As if sensing the tension between the two, Madame le Bret moved her wheelchair forward to Mia's hand. 'Have you ever done underwater swimming, my child?' she asked.

Mia turned to her gratefully. 'No, never.'

The old lady beamed. 'This then is a good opportunity. Gideon is an expert. He will teach you, won't you, *mon petit choux*,' she said with a chuckle.

Mia caught her breath. 'I'm sure Gideon wouldn't want to . . . I mean, I expect he'll be busy . . .'

He grinned, 'I'm on holiday, don't forget, Mia.'

'But I haven't a clue . . . I mean, it would be frightfully boring for you.' Mia stumbled over the words, uncomfortably aware that the amusement in Gideon's eyes was growing with each clumsy sentence she made.

'On the contrary,' he said dryly, 'I shall find it most amusing. Tomorrow morning at ten, be ready for me.'

'You will love it, my child,' Madame le Brett said. 'Do not be afraid. Gideon is a strong swimmer and he will give you protection.'

'Don't worry,' Gideon said, 'Mia is an excellent swimmer, except when she laughs underwater and comes up choking.'

'Oh!' Mia gasped. So he had been watching her that day on the beach! What had she laughed about? she wondered. Then she remembered. She had wondered if Gideon was afraid she was chasing him and that was why he avoided her.

She must have smiled, for Gideon looked at her now, one eyebrow raised above the other. 'Share the joke.'

'It was nothing.'

'You've gone bright red and have tears in your eyes,' Gideon said. 'As I've not hit you and so you're not in pain, it must be the tears of laughter. Why can't you tell us?'

'Gideon,' his grandmother scolded, 'you have embarrassed the poor girl. Let her be. It is her joke. Sometimes one laughs at something it is impossible to share.'

Mia touched the old lady's hand gently. 'That's it exactly, Madame le Bret,' she said gratefully, 'it's a joke I can't share.' She stood up. 'I think, if you'll excuse me, I'll go to bed,' she said, glancing at Gideon. 'I can see I shall need all my strength tomorrow.'

Gideon's chuckle followed her as she hurried indoors, but it was a friendly appreciative chuckle, so she did not mind.

*   *   *

She was ready at ten minutes to ten in the morning. She had chosen a black one-piece swimsuit, glad of her careful sun-tanning so that there were no white patches on her body. Gideon came out of the study, gave her a quick glance, saw that she was wearing rope-soled sandals and that she had a big towel.

He smiled. 'All set?'

It was such a pleasant friendly smile that Mia nearly tripped over one of the small tables. It was a smile impossible to describe, except by saying that it seemed to send out waves that warmed Mia and lightened the nervousness she had felt.

'Come on,' he said, holding out his hand.

It seemed the most natural thing in the world to walk down to the lagoon, Gideon holding her hand, swinging it, as he talked.

By the water's edge, he had the equipment ready. He talked as he helped Mia adjust the apparatus, telling her what to do, what not to do, and then they walked into the water.

Mia wondered afterwards of what she had been afraid. Not once did Gideon laugh at her or even tease her. He was considerate, appreciative, and always so friendly. She had never enjoyed swimming so much, nor had she ever had any idea of the totally new world into which she had suddenly plunged.

It made her feel lighter than air—and was the strangest sensation imaginable as she moved through the water. She could see Gideon by her side, his arms and legs waving like palm fronds in a slight breeze. As they reached the bottom of the lagoon, Gideon took her hand in his and they walked along with light, springy steps. There was so much to see—the tiny fish—and their slow twisting movements as they swam. She loved to see the way they played, almost like puppies chasing one another. Never had she seen such vivid vermilion, such a deep blue, a startling purple, and overwhelming orange.

When they surfaced, it was good to breathe in the fresh air. The sun blazed down out of the cloudless blue sky but the huge palm trees, slanting over the lagoon gave them shade. They sat on the rocks and Gideon lit a cigarette and passed it to her. They sat for a while in companionable silence and Mia felt relaxed completely. Never had Gideon been such fun, treating her like an equal, sharing something with her.

'Like it?' he asked.

She turned to smile at him, not knowing how her face sparkled in the sunshine for tiny drops of water still clung to her skin—or that her swept-back, still-wet hair added beauty to her high delicately moulded cheek-bones. Nor that her eyes were warm and she had the innocent happy look of a child.

'It was wonderful,' she said. 'I loved every moment of it. It's so different—I mean, it's like living in another world.'

Suddenly he was holding both her hands tightly, gazing at her as if he had never seen her before. His grey eyes were narrowed, a puzzled look on his face.

Mia caught her breath, trying to control the

shivers that always possessed her when Gideon touched her. Why was he looking at her like that?

And as suddenly, he dropped her hands, turning away, fumbling for a cigarette, lighting it. 'Promise me . . .' he said over his shoulder and his voice, too, had changed. It was harsh. 'Promise me you'll never do this alone.'

Hurt and bewildered by his change of mood, Mia said: 'But I'm a good swimmer.'

He swung round and his eyes were cold. 'It has nothing to do with your ability to swim,' he said stiffly. 'The point is—it can be dangerous unless you're with someone. You could get cramp—some of these innocent-looking fish have barbs whose poison can kill instantly.'

He stood up and Mia stood, too. They were only a few inches apart and he was still staring at her strangely, she thought.

'I must ask you, Mia,' he said coldly, 'to give me your word that you will never swim under water alone.'

Her cheeks felt on fire. 'I'm perfectly capable of taking care of myself!'

'That's the whole point. You're not. If you were, you wouldn't flare up like this the moment anyone tries to give you an inkling of what common sense is,' Gideon said icily. 'You are a good swimmer, granted. You can swim in the lagoon as much as you like, there are no dangerous currents there. But underwater swimming is a different cup of tea. I want your

133

word.'

Mia stared at him. Why had he to spoil everything? she thought unhappily. This need of his to be arrogant, to be the great big noise, the one who issued orders. She stifled a sigh. The magic of the morning had vanished.

She turned away to pick up her towel. 'I promise,' she said dully, and walked up to the house alone.

At lunch, Madame le Bret was eager to hear how Mia had enjoyed herself.

'It was wonderful,' Mia said, 'the fish are fantastic—such beautiful colours.'

The old lady beamed. 'I knew you would enjoy yourself. This afternoon,' she went on, 'I have a small bridge drive. I know that you don't care for the game, so I have asked three people. Perhaps you would amuse her, Gideon.'

'I can imagine nothing I would enjoy more,' Gideon said gravely, but Mia heard the sarcasm in his voice.

She glanced at him quickly and saw to her horror that he was laughing at her. Hastily she lifted the glass of wine that was always served with every meal and tried to hide her dismay in it. Had she shown her feelings too obviously?

'There's no need . . .' she said hastily, gulping down the wine and ending up with a coughing fit which, by the time she had controlled it with the aid of a pat on the back from Gideon, she saw had amused him even more. 'I can amuse myself,' she managed to say.

'I've got to see Reg Haseldine about some business,' Gideon said. 'I expect Phoebe would like to see you. She gets pretty lonely, you know.'

That wouldn't be so bad, Mia thought. 'I'd like that,' she told him.

'I'm delighted to please you,' said Gideon, and this time his sarcasm was too obvious for Madame le Bret not to notice.

She glanced at Mia's flushed cheeks and then at Gideon. 'Gideon, behave yourself,' the old lady said sharply. 'You make this dear child so unhappy, she will leave us.'

'Perhaps that's what I'm trying to do,' Gideon said.

'Gideon!' his grandmother said in such a shocked voice that he stood, went to her, bent down and kissed her.

'I apologise, Grand'mère . . . and to you, Mia. The joke was in bad taste,' he said. 'My teasing gets out of hand at times.'

Later, Mia went to her room to change. The humid heat of the island was never overwhelming, but she found herself changing her frocks several times a day. She thought of the afternoon ahead and she wished she had not agreed to go.

She liked Phoebe Haseldine so much—but if she was her mother, Mia thought worriedly, then perhaps she should go back to England as soon as possible, for if Reg found out, he would make Phoebe's life more miserable than ever.

Mia, ready in her green chiffon blouse and white pleated skirt, went out to the waiting carriage and was welcomed by a big smile from Pen. Gideon, in white shorts and a white shirt, long white socks and shining brown shoes, leapt out of the carriage to help Mia in with exaggerated courtesy.

'You should wear green more often, Mia,' he said.

Mia stared at him, startled by the friendliness of his voice. Had he already forgotten that little fight on the beach about her promise not to swim under water alone— or the little scene at lunchtime? Did the quarrels mean so little to him that he never even remembered them? Was she being foolish to let them annoy her? If only, she thought, she could learn to take them in her stride, to treat them as an amusing joke. If only he didn't have the power to make her feel so angry with him . . .

Mia and Phoebe sat on the terrace. From the open french windows behind them, they could hear the drone of voices; and occasionally pick out the whining tone of Reg, or the brisk authoritative voice of Gideon.

Phoebe looked happier. 'Gideon is a darling,' she said to Mia, as she sipped ice-cold, mint-flavoured drinks. 'He's found a reporter who wants to write up Reg's life. Now he's going to talk Reg into it—not an easy job, but Gideon always does succeed.'

'He never fails,' Mia said, and with, to her, rather surprising bitterness: 'He's indomitable—imperious.'

Phoebe, her hair untidy, her blue dress faded but very clean, looked at Mia oddly. 'You're engaged to be married, aren't you?' she asked.

Mia hesitated—but if she lied to Gideon, she must lie to everyone. She was beginning to wish she had told Gideon the truth, even though it would have meant suffering his sarcastic triumphant remarks.

'Yes—why?' It was so easy to talk to Phoebe, Mia thought.

Phoebe leant forward, lowering her voice. 'I was just going to say don't fall in love with Gideon, Mia.'

Mia stared at her, startled. 'Me—in love with Gideon?' she began to laugh. 'Phoebe,' she said, 'if you knew how much I hate him!'

The french windows behind her closed abruptly. The thick net curtains, that shut out the sunlight Reg Haseldine refused to enjoy, also shut out the form of whoever was shutting the windows, but Mia realised with a start it could only be Gideon. For a moment, her heart seemed to skip a beat, but then she could laugh. What did it matter if Gideon—arrogant, ruthless, conceited Gideon—did learn the truth?

'You hate him?' Phoebe said slowly. 'But how could anyone hate a man like Gideon?'

Mia's face felt on fire. 'Well, I do . . . sometimes,' she said defiantly.

It was Phoebe's turn to laugh. 'Ah, that makes it different, Mia. Gideon can be infuriating at times, the way he teases. Does that get your goat?'

Mia nodded; suddenly her eyes were stinging. 'Sometimes he says such cruel things,' she said, and had to stop, her voice unsteady.

Phoebe took Mia's hand in hers gently. 'Listen, Mia, you must try to understand Gideon. He was brought up very strictly. He is the most ethical man I know, but he can be intolerant. There are only two colours for Gideon—black and white. Grey doesn't exist. I mean by that that he sees right and wrong, nothing else. He has no use for weakness, no tolerance for failure or cowardice. He is a perfectionist. He expects terrific high standards of other people because that's the way he lives. We often fail him and then he's hurt, and his hurt makes him angry. He can't realise that we're not all Gideon Eastwoods.'

'Thanks be!' Mia murmured rebelliously, and then found herself smiling at Phoebe's amused face. 'I know I shouldn't let it get me down, Phoebe,' she confessed, 'but . . . but Gideon said some terrible things about my — about Ian. He said he was weak and a mother's boy.'

'And is he?' Phoebe asked quietly.

Mia nodded, unable to speak for a moment. Whatever happened, Gideon must not find her in tears. Imagine the scathing remarks he would make!

'So you're angry with him for telling you the truth? Perhaps he thought you should know, Mia. It might be that he was worried about you—that it was for your future happiness, that he told you the truth.'

'But it's none of his business,' Mia began.

Phoebe smiled and shook her head. 'Gideon thinks it is. He'd slay me if he heard this, but Gideon is a natural "do-gooder." These days, people are inclined to sneer at those who help others, to call them soft or dopes—but Gideon is one of those people who are, quite naturally, their brother's keeper. Gideon has helped more people unostentatiously and with no desire for gratitude than anyone I know. When I think of how he has helped us—and the Contessa. You've met her?'

'Yes. I find it difficult to talk to her.'

Phoebe sighed. 'Don't we all? Poor creature, I feel so sorry for her. At least she had her child for several years . . .' she added sadly.

Mia was filled with an intense desire to throw her arms round Phoebe and tell her the truth. Or the truth as she believed it must be—that she was Phoebe's child. She was the baby

Phoebe had to give up, for the baby's sake. She was the child, grown into woman, to whom every year Phoebe sent a birthday present, the child she had not been allowed to keep, the child she yearned for. They would have to keep it a secret from everyone, especially from Gideon. He would probably think it his duty to tell Reg the truth, in order that Phoebe might openly enjoy her motherhood. Gideon would have no patience with Reg's jealous possessiveness. He would expect Reg to accept this strange girl as his step-daughter, but could they keep it a secret? The temptation was so great that she had to think wildly for something to say to change the conversation.

'Did you know Madeleine Fox well?' Mia asked abruptly.

'Madeleine Foxer . . .?' Phoebe said, her attention diverted successfully. 'Of course, I knew her very well. I was sorry when she left the island.'

Mia leaned forward. 'What was she like? How old was she? I believe she was a widow?'

'That's right. She came here to get over it. It took three years. She was a very nice person. About my age.'

'Your age?' said Mia, her thoughts whirling. 'Had she children? Or had she had children?'

'I don't think so. She rarely talked about the past at all,' Phoebe said thoughtfully. 'I always had the feeling, though, that it wasn't only the death of her husband she was grieving about. I

140

felt there had been another tragedy in her life, much earlier. But she hardly talked at all of her married life. Just that they weren't very happy and she often thought it was her fault, for she had lived in the past too much.'

'What was she like?' Mia asked. 'D'you know where she went?'

'She was tall and very thin. Attractive in a model's type of way. Very long legs. She looked super in any clothes. Fair-haired. Yes, I have her address. We do write occasionally.'

The windows behind Mia were pushed open. She was startled, for she had not heard them open earlier, but as Gideon stepped out she wondered if he had left them partly open on purpose to see what else she would say about him.

'Reg thinks it's a good idea, Phoebe,' Gideon said, ignoring Mia completely. 'I'll cable home and get Mike Harvey out as soon as possible . . .' He grinned. 'In other words, before Reg changes his mind.'

For one awful moment, Mia thought Phoebe was going to cry as she clung to Gideon's arm. 'How can I thank you?'

He touched her cheek lightly. 'By smiling more, Phoebe. Ready, Mia?' he added curtly.

Driving home in the carriage, Pen's back very straight, his ears pricked, Mia wondered why Gideon spoke so little. Not that she minded, for she had so much to think of. Was she jumping to conclusions when she thought

Phoebe was her mother? she wondered. Could this Madeleine Foxer be her mother, instead? 'A tragedy in the past.' 'Living too much in the past.' 'Grieving for more than a dead husband.' It could all add up, Mia thought. Three years on the island, too. If only she had taken her father's advice and waited until her birthday. The postmark on her parcel would have told her if her real mother was still on the Isle d'Amour. Now she was fumbling in the dark, picking up a clue here, losing a clue there.

As they went into the house, Mia jumped as Gideon barked—no other word could describe the way he spoke, she thought—at her. 'I want to speak to you alone in my study. Come in fifteen minutes,' he added curtly as he walked straight to his room.

Showering, changing into her blue chiffon dinner frock, Mia only wondered vaguely what Gideon had to say to her that could not be said aloud in the carriage, for she was too busy thinking about Madeleine Foxer.

The soft sweet music Madame le Bret loved filled the house as Mia walked to Gideon's study, knocking, waiting for him to speak before going in. He was busy writing a letter, but he looked up and told her curtly to sit down.

She obeyed, glancing round the monastically simple study. It was very businesslike—great steel filing cabinets, two

142

tape recorders, a bookcase of technical books he obviously often used. His head was bent over the letter he was writing, so she had time to study him.

What a strange man he was. Such a mixture of moods. So able to make people admire, respect and even love him, she thought. How could any girl in her right mind, who was loved by a man like Gideon, jilt him for another man? Mia's eyes narrowed as she studied his short thick dark hair, the strong nose, the stubborn chin. It was hard to imagine Gideon hurt—he was too strong to be as human as that. Yet his grandmother had said how vulnerable he was, how easily hurt.

And Phoebe had said Gideon felt he was 'his brother's keeper', that he was constrained to help people, Mia thought.

She remembered Phoebe's warning: 'Don't fall in love with Gideon,' she had said. Mia knew better than to be such a fool. Any girl loving Gideon was asking for trouble, she told herself. He expected and demanded so much—could any human woman be all that Gideon would expect of her? No, she told herself again, very firmly, that whatever happened, there was one thing she was not going to do—and that was to fall in love with Gideon.

'Well?' Gideon asked suddenly.

Mia was startled. She blinked, her long lashes framing her green eyes, looking at

143

Gideon.

'Satisfied?' he asked. 'You've been sitting there staring at me for quite a while.' Even as her cheeks glowed, he added: 'Not that I've the right to criticise you, for I know I'm always staring at you.'

'You said you wanted to see me about something,' Mia said formally.

'Oh yes.' Gideon seemed to hesitate. 'Why do you ask so many questions, Mia?' he demanded abruptly, seeing her surprise, and continuing before she could answer.

'Today—at Phoebe's. It was all about Madeleine Foxer. She had gone long before you heard about the island, so why all the curiosity? I hear the same everywhere. You're so interested in everything to do with the island and its inhabitants. Pen said you asked more questions than any woman he'd ever met . . .' For a moment Gideon smiled. 'Pen likes it, so that was no complaint. But all the same, Mia, why do you ask questions?'

She drew a long deep breath and stared at him. 'Because I want the answers?' she said lightly. 'Or because I'm plain curious? Maybe it's the latter. I like to know about people, and . . .'

'Baloney,' Gideon interrupted rudely. 'There must be a reason. Are you over here looking for something?'

The question was so near the truth that Mia felt as if everything inside her stood still for a moment, afraid to move or even breathe. If Gideon guessed the truth . . .

She managed a little laugh. 'What could I be looking for?'

He rested his chin on his hand, elbow on desk, and frowned. 'I don't know.'

'So . . .' she said, and gave a little shrug.

There was a silence and then Gideon asked: 'Are you planning to write a book about us?'

Mia began to laugh. 'Oh, Gideon, do I look like a writer?'

'Then what is it?'

Mia had regained her confidence. For once she was handling Gideon well. 'Maybe I'm a spy,' she said gaily.

He stood up. 'Even that wouldn't surprise me, Mia. You've such a deceptively innocent look when all the time you are really very ingenious.' He took her arm and led her to the door. 'But please be a little more mature in your behaviour, Mia. I'd hate you to be called the local Prying Paul.'

Deftly he put her outside the door and closed it so that she stood in the hall alone.

At least she had saved the situation— Gideon had not wormed the truth out of her. Prying Paul, indeed! she thought. Trust Gideon to find the most unkind name for it.

*   *   *

Mia pleaded a headache next morning and had

her breakfast in bed. By the time she was dressed and had joined Madame le Bret, Gideon had vanished, she was glad to see. She spent the morning with the old lady, helping her water her beloved cuttings. When Gideon joined them for lunch, Mia was coldly formal with him, barely addressing him, so that she was startled when his invitation came as they were sitting on the terrace, watching two small pirogues out in the lagoon.

'One of my men is flying over today, Mia. Like to come to the air-strip with me?' Gideon asked.

Startled, Mia turned, trying to think of an excuse, but Madame le Bret answered for her: 'I'm sure she would, Gideon. I don't think she's seen your bubble-plane yet.'

'Bubble-plane?' Mia echoed.

Gideon laughed, taking her cup to refill it for her from the beautiful Queen Anne silver coffee pot. 'That's what Grand'mère calls my helicopter.'

'Have you got one here?'

'Yes, and very useful it can be too,' Gideon told her. 'Some of the few tourists we suffer from get lost at times—they will climb the mountains at the north end of the island and there are few roads there and no transport available at all. Then I go up in my helicopter, find them, and bring them back.'

Mia's eyes widened. 'That sounds wonderful!'

'Not wonderful,' he said dryly, 'just plain sensible. I can haul them up—if they're not too badly injured—or can land practically on a square of ground. One day I'll take you up, if you like.'

'I would. I've never been up in a helicopter.'

The journey to the air-strip was leisurely, old Nero ambling along, Pen twisted on his seat, so that he could chat with Gideon, Mia content to be quiet and look around her.

Had there ever been so beautiful a place? she wondered, as the road twisted and turned. Every now and then through a clearing in the trees, she would catch glimpses of the blue water or the white sands. Looking the other way, she could see the great mountain towering above the island, making it appear so thin and narrow by contrast. The mountain was three thousand feet high, Gideon had told her. He had also said they were just below the Equator. From the mountaintop, he had told her, they could see the Indian Ocean rolling away on every side, and only distant green smudges to tell them that the islands were not so far away.

*   *   *

At the air-strip, Gideon vanished, but first he directed Pen to show Mia the helicopter. Dutifully Pen obeyed and with Mia walked round it, Pen explaining at great length all he knew about the machine. Later, Gideon joined them and let Mia sit inside.

'I think I'd feel frightfully insecure,' she said, looking out at the two men.

'With me?' Gideon asked, his eyes amused. 'I thought I was Indomitable, Indestructible and Impossible.'

Mia hesitated and suddenly she laughed. 'You are—all of those,' she said, and he helped her out.

They sat on chairs taken from the big hangar, and put under the shady trees at the end of the strip. Gideon consulted his watch.

'We'll hear them . . .' he began, and stopped as the sound of a plane broke up the quietness. 'Good, they're on time.'

'Who's coming out, Gideon?' Mia asked. She was wearing a yellow frock. Ever since Gideon had made that unusual remark that she should always wear green, something had kept her from wearing anything that was green. She didn't want him to think she was wearing green because he admired it, or because he had insinuated—for she could think of no other explanation for his remark— that green suited her. It would make life absolutely unbearable if Gideon ever thought she was making a play for him.

'A chap named Walter King,' said Gideon, shading his eyes against the sun, looking up at the speck in the sky that came closer and larger every second. 'He's in his mid-twenties,

148

but quite bright. I'm grooming him for a top job in the firm. I can only stay out here so long if I'm in constant touch. Cables and letters are useless, so I'm having Walter fly out regularly to give me the know-how.'

Mia stared at him, shaking her head slowly. How incredibly, terribly wealthy he must be—or else how prosperous the firm. When she thought of the cost of her flight . . . It was like the grip of an icy hand closing round her heart.

'Gideon,' she said so sharply, that he turned at once. Her hand had flown to her mouth. 'I've just remembered I never paid you for my fare out.'

He looked amused. 'So what? Don't sound so tragic.'

'But what must you have thought of me?'

'I didn't even think of it. Gwyneth got the tickets for me and it never entered my head.'

'But I must pay you,' Mia said desperately. She was in debt to him for so much, she could not bear to owe him money as well.

He was looking at the plane as it slowly circled the island. 'Don't fret, Mia. If you really want to pay, I'll get Gwyneth to send you an account and you can send her a cheque.'

'You won't forget?'

He gave an odd little laugh. 'From the sound of your voice, you won't let me forget.' He turned and took hold of her by the shoulders, staring down at her. 'Mia, why do you hate me so much?' he asked.

She stared up at him, her mouth suddenly dry. She shivered and he frowned. 'You're not really scared of me, are you?' he asked.

'Of course not . . . it's just . . . Mia began, but some-one shouted and the roar of the plane came closer above their heads as the plane circled to land. Gideon's hands left her shoulders as he turned to watch the plane land. The door was opened and someone was helped out.

'Good grief!' Gideon said softly.

Mia saw by his expression that he was annoyed. As she turned to watch the plane, she saw that it was a woman who had got out and was waving at them.

'Gwyneth Vaughan!' Gideon exclaimed as, ignoring Mia, he began to walk towards the plane.

Mia hurried by his side, not sure what to do, but not wanting to stand alone like a puppet.

'You didn't expect her?'

Gideon turned to stare at her. 'I most certainly did not,' he said.

And then Gwyneth was coming to meet them. Mia caught her breath. She had only seen Gideon's personal assistant once before, but then she had thought she was beautiful— but today she looked incredibly lovely.

Gwyneth was tall and slender as a wand, she was wearing a beautifully cut suit of crimson silk, her dark hair gleaming in the sun, her beautiful face flushed with excitement.

'Gideon!' she exclaimed, holding out both her hands, her deep red handbag swinging on a silver chain from one wrist. 'It's so good to see you.'

He was gazing past her. 'Walter King?'

'His wife was sick, they're expecting their first baby, you know, Gideon. My holiday was due and you're always saying I should come out here to relax, so I thought I'd kill two birds with one stone. I've got all the data you need, so I can get you up to date,' Gwyneth told him.

She looked past Gideon at Mia and her thin black eyebrows arched. 'Why, hullo, Miss Barton, are you still here?'

'Hullo,' Mia said. 'Yes, I am.'

Gwyneth was not listening. She had tucked her hand through Gideon's arm and was leading the way to the carriage and Nero. Pen was standing by the horse's head, a most peculiar look on his face, Mia saw.

'Gideon, please don't be mad at me,' Gwyneth was saying, looking up at the tall man. 'I had a bad time these last few weeks, and then spring collapsed and we had snow. Imagine it—snow at this time of year! I felt if I don't get some sunshine soon, I'll go mad. Say you don't mind . . .'

'Of course I don't mind,' Gideon said slowly. 'It's just that my orders were . . .'

'I know—I know. I also know how you dislike your orders being ignored, Gideon, but what could I do? I only did what I knew you would do. I gave Walter three weeks' leave. His wife's in hospital and they're very worried, as something has gone wrong. I knew that was what you'd do. It seemed most sensible after the expense of flying me out, if I took my holiday now.'

'Most logical,' Gideon said dryly.

He helped Gwyneth into the carriage. Mia noticed that neither Gwyneth nor Pen had looked at one another. Gideon stood back and turned to Mia with a smile.

'I'll sit with Pen,' she said.

Gideon frowned. 'You most certainly won't,' he said quietly, and practically lifted her into the carriage.

Gwyneth was looking round her. 'Isn't this delightfully primitive, Miss Barton? Like moving back two generations. You must be awfully bored here without friends of your own age.'

'On the contrary,' Gideon said quietly, 'Mia has made a lot of friends. My grandmother and she get on well together.'

Gwyneth flashed him a radiant smile. 'Oh, they would, of course, Gideon. Madame le Bret adores anyone young.'

Nero was ambling along slowly. Pen's back was hunched, his coat collar, despite the heat, turned up, as if he wanted to shut out sounds from behind.

'You've still got . . .' said Gwyneth, jerking her head at Pen. 'Gideon, you're too soft. I'm always telling you so, aren't I?'

'Yes, you are,' Gideon agreed.

Mia sat very still, her hands clasped as she looked blindly out of the carriage. What had happened to her? she wondered. Why this terrible raging frightening anger that was speeding through her? So what if Gideon did love Gwyneth? There could be no other reason for his meek acceptance of her behaviour. But it was no business of Mia's!

Look at the way Gwyneth talked to him, Mia told herself. Why, if *she* had spoken like that, Gideon would have torn her apart with sarcastic remarks. Look how meekly he was letting Gwyneth lecture him on the subject that while it was good to live peacefully, their life on the island would be improved if he allowed a few amenities to come.

'In a car, you'd be home in minutes . . . not what seems like hours,' Gwyneth said scornfully.

Mia closed her eyes tightly; she was feeling most peculiar. As the carriage jerked and swayed, she was thrown against Gideon's bare arm every few seconds. Each time it was as if she had an electric shock—it went right through her. She no longer saw the palm trees, the oleanders, the cream-flowered frangipani—nor Pen's back or Nero's head in its funny little straw hat. All she knew was that Gideon was next to her, his flesh touching her flesh—and, the most awful part of it all was that to Gideon, she did not exist.

There was only Gwyneth.

CHAPTER SEVEN

As Gwyneth was helped out of the carriage, she looked up at Gideon with a smile. 'My usual room?' she asked.

He shook his head. 'No. I'll arrange something for you. Mia is in that room.'

'Mia . . .?' Gwyneth echoed, looking puzzled. And then she turned to look at Mia. 'Oh! You mean Miss Barton? She's staying with you?' Gwyneth sounded shocked, and Mia's cheeks suddenly burned.

'Yes, the guest house wasn't able to take her, we found, when we got here,' Gideon said casually, 'so she stayed with us, and when the guest house re-opened we asked Mia to stay on.'

Gideon led the way into the cool hall, fragrant with scent from the many flowers, and perhaps, Mia thought, he did not see the fury on Gwyneth Vaughan's face as she turned to look at Mia, as if about to speak.

But Gideon also turned before she could say anything, took Mia by the arm and said: 'Grand'mère will be waking up about now, Mia. Would you tell her we have a visitor? She likes to know beforehand.'

The pressure of Gideon's fingers on Mia's arms should have warned her in advance, but she was quite unprepared for Madame le Bret's very real dismay.

'But the one time I have Gideon to myself, she must come. Why did he not tell me? He was ashamed? He knows that Miss Vaughan and I are like two cats sparring for a fight . . .' Madame le Bret sat up in bed, leaning against pillows so that she was completely relaxed, but now her face seemed to crumple. 'Oh, why must he do this to me?'

Mia held her hand tightly. 'But he didn't, Madame le Bret. He had no idea . . .' she began, and then told the old lady about Gideon's surprise and annoyance at the airstrip.

Madame let Bret seemed more cheerful then. 'But why does she come here for a holiday? She is always so bored, though she tries to hide it from Gideon. You have not met her before?'

'Once. In London, when I went to ask Gideon for a lift.'

Madame le Bret's eyes began to twinkle. 'Ah—now this I understand. She knew that Gideon was bringing you out? I see now why she has come. In London, Paris, New York—everywhere but on Isle d'Amour, Miss Vaughan is Gideon's right hand. He respects and admires her, he finds her invaluable, but here—she is not at her best! It would have to be something urgent to bring her here, to risk disillusioning him. But jealousy gives courage.'

'But she couldn't be jealous of me,' protested Mia. 'She's so incredibly beautiful.'

'And you?' the little old lady chuckled. 'Are you the ugly duckling? The one with a big face and bow legs?' she teased. 'You have beauty of a much more lasting nature than Miss Vaughan's. Hers comes out of little pots and tubes.'

'But Gideon . . .' Mia hesitated. 'People on the island think that Gideon is in love with the Countess.'

Madame le Bret sobered and let Mia help her off the bed and into her wheelchair. 'That is what I fear—but Miss Vaughan is also a danger. Here I can keep an eye on Gideon, but when he is thousands of miles away . . .' She gave a little helpless shrug.

'But if Gideon loves one of them . . . ?'

'My child, love is a strange thing,' Madame le Bret said sadly. 'We can all be deceived. I had hoped . . . when I saw you . . . but then I saw your ring and knew that you belonged to another man. I can still hope . . .' Her face was bright with mischief. 'Have you any idea how often Gideon stares at you? There is something in your face that intrigues him, that is like a magnet, he cannot tear away his eyes.'

Mia laughed as she gently undid the pins in the old lady's hair. 'May I brush it for you?' she asked. 'Gideon only stares at me,' she went on, 'because I remind him of someone.'

Madame le Bret, in her cream silk negligée, ran her hand through her thin white hair and laughed. 'That is what he says, my child. Men are good at making excuses. Yes, I would be happy if you brush my hair.'

When Mia went to join Gideon on the terrace, having defiantly changed into a green frock, she saw that Gwyneth, who had changed into an incredibly attractive pair of white slacks with an embroidered azure-blue silk blouse, was annoyed.

'But my first evening, Gideon,' she was saying. 'You can't walk out on me!'

Mia stood in the doorway, half hidden by the golden silk curtains, but Gideon turned to her.

'Everything under control, Mia?' he asked.

She went out reluctantly and sat down. 'Everything.'

Gwyneth crossed her long slender legs and ignored Mia completely. 'But, Gideon, you know how your grandmother dislikes me . . .'

'I had a feeling it was mutual,' he said dryly.

'I never know what to talk to old people about,' Gwyneth said, opening her white mesh handbag, pulling out a jade green cigarette holder and waiting while Gideon put a cigarette in it for her, and then lit it with his gold lighter. 'Nor very young ones,' she added, with a quick unfriendly glance at Mia.

Gideon chuckled. 'Well, it's your own fault,

Gwyneth. I'd no idea you'd be here tonight and I made this date some time ago. If you prefer it, you can have dinner served in your room.'

Mia listened in dismay. Was she to entertain Gwyneth Vaughan alone that evening? she wondered, for she had a horrible feeling that Madame le Bret would suddenly have a headache so that she could retire with dignity.

'Who are you dining with?' Gwyneth asked.

Mia caught her breath and glanced at Gideon. It was not the sort of question she could ever ask him. But she saw he did not mind.

'The Contessa,' he said casually.

'The Contessa!' Gwyneth echoed. That was all, but it was the way she said it that annoyed Mia. 'I suppose she's still feeling sorry for herself and making you all miserable. Can't you put it off?'

'I don't want to,' said Gideon.

Gwyneth stared at him and then suddenly she was laughing. 'Gideon, you're an absolute . . .! Honestly! The way you behave. Just because you're annoyed with me for turning up without warning . . .'

Gideon was laughing, too. 'So long as you get the message, Gwyn.' He stood up. 'Care for a stroll down to the lagoon?' He glanced at Mia. 'Like to join us?'

Quickly she shook her head. 'I think I'll go and see how Madame le Bret is. She had a bit of a headache . . .' Mia improvised, and saw the laughter in Gideon's eyes. He, too, knew that his grandmother would probably dine in bed that night.

Mia watched them walk across the lawn. Gwyneth had brushed her hair and then twisted it in a loose coil on the nape of her neck. Her skin was magnolia-creamy, her dark eyes flashing as she glanced up at Gideon, her hand resting lightly on his arm as they talked. Gideon was laughing, shaking his head, and Gwyneth suddenly stood still, turned, put both hands on Gideon's arms and stared up at him, obviously asking a question. Gideon bent forward . . . and Mia jumped up, hurrying into the house, not glancing back, not wishing to see Gideon take Gwyneth in his arms to kiss her.

Safely inside the house, she stood still. Was that pounding her heart? Why was she so upset about Gwyneth's arrival? Her possessiveness towards Gideon, his acceptance of her behaviour. It was as if there was some secret understanding between them—as if they could say things to one another and know they were not meant.

Feeling desolate, Mia went in search of Madame le Bret.

'Gideon's dining with the Contessa,' she said.

Madame le Bret had chosen to wear a very glamorous, as Mia told her, gown of cream lace. For a moment she looked horrified and then she chuckled.

'Don't look so worried, dear child,' she said. 'I will immediately phone some of my friends and say that we have an unexpected—' her eyes twinkled—'I will not be unkind and say "uninvited" guest. That way we need not talk to her.'

Mia had to laugh. 'You're wonderful, Madame le Bret,' she said, stooping to kiss the old lady's cheek.

'Just sensible, my child. I am accustomed to these disconcerting incidents. You will see, my dear, how well it works.'

How right she was, Mia found, later that evening as four couples came to dine. Gwyneth Vaughan was treated by everyone with a rather exaggerated fuss, but she obviously enjoyed it. She had changed into a sheath of red and orange which was, Madame le Bret whispered to Mia, alarmingly eye-catching.

'It is as well,' Madame le Bret said softly, 'that Gideon is out tonight.'

But Gideon came home early—for the Contessa did not keep late hours—and Mia saw the look on his face as he stood in the doorway and stared at Gwyneth.

She was standing in front of a carved black screen, the darkness throwing up the colour of the gown that clung so gently to her slender body as she talked to the elderly man who was

160

laughing at something she said. Mia looked at Gwyneth's slender waist, the graceful movements of her head, the vivacity in her beautiful face . . . and then looked again at Gideon.

He was walking across the room towards Gwyneth, seeing no one else, just making for her, as if drawn by a magnet that could not be defied. And it was as if Gwyneth felt or sensed his approach, for she turned abruptly and looked at him. She, too, had apparently forgotten everyone else as she walked to meet him.

Mia slipped away. No one would miss her. In her own room, she stood for a while in darkness and then went to the window, sliding back the mosquito screen. She could see the tall palm trees with their slow graceful movements—hear the rustle of their fronds and the distant roar of the surf.

She rested her hot face against the glass as she faced the truth.

She loved Gideon.

Oh no, she thought wildly, it mustn't— it couldn't—be true. Stop it at once, she told herself angrily. This is imagination. Infatuation. A passing interest.

But it was useless. And she knew it. What she had always told herself could never happen had! She was in love with Gideon.

She closed the screen, drew the blinds, switched on the light and glared at her pale-faced, shocked reflection. Now look what you've done, she said to herself angrily.

But it was too late. What was the good of being angry with herself—or with anyone? It's too late, she repeated to herself; now all she could do was to hide her love for him. No one—but no one at all—must ever be allowed to guess.

As the days passed, Mia saw little of Gideon, and certainly was never alone with him. Gwyneth saw to that!

Gwyneth was never actually rude to her, but there are subtle ways of shutting a person out—and Gwyneth was an expert at them. She would talk to Gideon about people they had met, or about business, or some incident in the past, so that Mia would feel ignored, out of the conversation, not only unable to join in, but knowing that she was what Madame le Bret, who seemed to grow more quiet and old with each day that passed, called *de trop*.

Gwyneth seemed to dominate the scene, just as Gideon did in his masculine way. No matter what dress Mia chose to wear, when she saw Gwyneth, she thought she might just as well have worn sackcloth! Gwyneth could get away with anything and still look beautiful, even in rather dramatic blue lace slacks with a matching, low-necked bodice. Her earrings were always huge, bizarrely carved, yet they suited her dramatic look. Maybe it was her silky black hair, her dark eyes, the lashes

Madame le Bret told Mia could only have come out of a box. But Gwyneth seemed to have everything.

'Except Gideon,' Madame le Bret said to Mia consolingly.

'Sometimes I think she's got him,' Mia said, and knew from the old lady's face that Gideon's grandmother had the same fear.

Gideon seemed to be enjoying his holiday—he had not teased Mia or been sarcastic since Gwyneth's arrival, Mia realised. Frequently, Mia and Madame le Bret did not see Gideon for hours, for he took Gwyneth sailing on his yacht and for a ride over the island in his helicopter which came low over the garden, buzzing noisily before lurching up again.

Mia lay on the sands alone and looked through dark glasses at the helicopter, thinking of Gideon and Gwyneth in there, alone together, and the ache inside her grew larger with every breath she drew.

Why, oh why had she to fall in love with Gideon? So long as no one guessed!

More and more often, as the days passed, Mia found herself dropping in to see Phoebe, who always welcomed her, even though Reg these days was more cheerful.

Phoebe was sympathetic about Gwyneth. 'I can't stand her, and I just don't see what Gideon can see in her. I'd say she was ruthless and hard. Maybe he likes her because people always turn to stare at her, and men like that—

until they're married,' she added, with a quick chuckle and a glance at her husband, who was lost in reading one of his newspaper cuttings. 'Also Gwyneth, let's face it, is intelligent.'

Mia tried to smile. 'Something we're not?'

Phoebe gave her a hug. 'I'm not, but maybe you are.'

Mia always enjoyed her visits to the Haseldines. With each visit, she felt more sure that Phoebe was her mother. If only, she thought, there was some way she could find out for certain. Once she tried to probe as she deliberately turned the conversation to holidays.

'I've always thought,' Mia said, 'I'd like to visit Spain. Have you been there, Phoebe?'

Phoebe looked up. 'Spain? Oh, yes, with Reg. I think we've been about everywhere in the world.'

'It must have been fun,' Mia said lamely, for it was not the answer she had hoped for.

One thing Mia disliked very much was Gwyneth's habit of sneering at the Contessa. ' "Moderate lamentation is the right of the dead," ' Gwyneth quoted once. ' "Exceeding grief the enemy to the living," is what Shakespeare said. Even if it was tragic, she should try to get over it. She's just spoiling everyone's pleasure.'

'It is not so easy when you are very sad,' Madame le Bret said gently.

Gwyneth looked across the dining table at

the old lady. 'But you can't go on grieving for ever.'

'Can't you?' Madame le Brett asked. 'She does not enjoy it, you know.'

Gwyneth, who was wearing black trousers and an orientally embroidered orange and white tunic, looked at her. 'Madame le Bret, you are so like Gideon—both so soft and kind-hearted you believe the best of everyone. I think the Contessa does enjoy it, it gives her drama, it makes people conscious and aware of her. So many widows and divorcees complain that no one notices them, they are redundant. The Contessa has solved that problem by making everyone sorry for her. Frankly, I think she revels in grief.'

'If you knew her as well as we do, Gwyneth,' Gideon said quietly, 'you'd know that was not true. We seek her out. She doesn't want to be dramatic, or have people make a fuss of her. Sometimes she hates us for trying to make her join us.'

Mia turned to look at him swiftly, grateful for his defence of the Contessa. How terribly handsome Gideon was, she thought with a little ache inside her. She particularly loved him in his evening clothes. The wide, scarlet cummerbund, the well-cut white jacket, the silk shirt suited him so well. He looked so completely happy . . .

Mia was startled when, much later that evening, Gideon sought her out. 'Mia,' he said, coming straight to the point, 'I need your help. D'you feel about the Contessa as Gwyneth does?'

They were standing on the terrace. Gwyneth had gone to her bedroom to get something and Madame le Bret had just retired to bed. It was beautifully quiet, the tall palms hardly moving in the hot evening air, the sweet scent of the flowers surrounding them as Mia stared at Gideon. It was the first time he had spoken to her alone for ages, she thought. And he needed her help!

'Of course I don't . . .' Mia began warmly, and then hesitated. Was that implying disapproval of his wonderful Gwyneth? she wondered uneasily. 'I'm very sorry for her, but . . .'

'You find it hard to be friends with her?'

Mia nodded. 'I never know what to talk to the Contessa about. I'm always afraid of saying the wrong thing.'

'I know,' said Gideon. He sighed wearily. 'But somehow we must break through that façade of indifference to mankind behind which she hides. She's a wonderful person, Mia. I wish you'd known her before the tragedy. She was so happy, so gay . . .'

How sad he sounded, Mia thought instantly. Were the people on the island right, she wondered, and was it the Contessa Gideon loved? And because the Contessa wanted nothing to do with anyone, was that why he

166

had turned to Gwyneth?

'Honestly, Gideon,' she said slowly, 'if there is anything I can do to help the Contessa, you know I'll gladly do it.'

His hand closed round her arm warmly. She clenched her hands, willing herself not to shiver, to stay still.

'I know, Mia, thanks . . .' Gideon was saying when Gwyneth sailed out of the house, giving one quick glance at Gideon's hand on Mia's arms.

'Those earrings of mine, Gideon, they've gone . . .' Gwyneth began, her voice accusing.

Gideon turned, forgetting Mia by his side. 'They can't just have gone, Gwyneth.'

'They have—and they cost a small fortune,' Gwyneth said.

'Where did you leave them?'

'On the dressing table. I was going to wear them, but they clashed with this tunic. They're not there now. Someone's stolen them!' Her voice rose hysterically.

'My dear girl,' Gideon said, walking towards her, 'Nothing has ever been stolen in this house. You've probably put them down somewhere and forgotten where they are.'

'I don't do things like that,' snapped Gwyneth.

Mia slipped past them quietly and into the house. Let them fight it out, she thought, but she was sure, like Gideon, that there had never been a thief in the house. Nor was there one now.

She stopped dead as she saw a shadow move quickly. 'Anna-Marie,' Mia said without thinking, recognising the little French maid.

The girl came out of the darkness and stood there, head hanging, tears running down her cheeks.

'I am not a thief . . .' she sobbed, speaking in French. 'I took them because they are so beautiful and just to show to my friends. Here they are . . .' She held out her hand and gave the earrings to Mia. 'She is so angry always, that—' Anna-Marie choked as she tried not to sob, 'everything I do is wrong. If she knew I had taken them . . . she would send me to prison. I was on my way to put them back and I heard her call me a thief . . .'

'Put them back where you found them, Anna-Marie,' Mia said gently. 'No one need know.'

The girl, in her black frock and crisp white pleated apron, shook her head. 'I am afraid. Should she find me, she would not believe me as you do.'

'I'll put them back, then,' said Mia, taking the earrings, turning back to make sure that Gwyneth was still in the garden.

There were only shaded lights on in the hall that led to the terrace and Mia had reached the silk curtains before she heard her name mentioned. Then she froze, the carved earrings digging into her hands as she clutched them.

'Gideon, Mia is chasing you. Can't you see it?' Gwyneth was saying, her voice low but not low enough. Mia could hear each word plainly. 'You're so soft, Gideon, so fooled by these innocent-eyed young people, but Mia is as hard as nails. The whole thing was planned from the beginning. It's so obvious!'

'What is obvious?' Gideon asked. Mia's hand went to her throat. How angry he sounded. With her? she wondered.

'That she chased you. You met her at that engagement party—she discovered where you lived . . .'

'She did not, Gwyneth,' Gideon said quietly. 'I remember clearly saying I lived on an island in the Indian Ocean.'

'Don't split hairs,' said Gwyneth. 'Are there so many in the Indian Ocean? You're a famous person, it wouldn't have been hard for her to discover on which island you lived. Nor to learn that you often give people lifts out here. I know her father died, I'm not suggesting she killed him, but I am suggesting that meeting you, she realised you'd be a better financial proposition than that weak-kneed Ian Yates, so she decided to make use of your soft heart. I wouldn't mind betting she lied about booking in at the guest house.'

'She didn't, Gwyneth,' said Gideon, his voice still quiet. 'I know from Phoebe.'

'Phoebe's probably on her side. All these

people are selfish, Gideon. You're too generous. I'm sorry for Ian—he's very much in love with Mia, and even if he is rather weak, we can't all be Gideon Eastwoods, can we?' she laughed. 'Seriously, though, Gideon, Mia seems so charming, but look at the way she's worked on your grandmother, making herself indispensable. These young people can be very clever, so watch out—or you'll end up with Mia for a wife!'

'Thanks for the warning, Gwyneth,' said Gideon, in a strange voice.

Mia wished she could see his face, the expression in his eyes. Did he really believe those lies of Gwyneth's? Could he think that she was capable of doing such a thing?

And yet, she thought, as she turned and slipped away, maybe he did. Hadn't he, at their very first meeting, accused her of marrying Ian for his money?

CHAPTER EIGHT

Three days later the invitation came. Mia was helping Madame le Bret arrange the flowers and they were talking about Reg's amazing reaction to the arrival of the English reporter who was going to write up his life.

'I think it was a wonderful idea of Gideon's,' Madame le Bret was saying as Gideon walked into the conservatory where the flowers were stacked on shelves, waiting for Madame's loving skilful hands to work on them.

'Oh, he has his ideas,' Gideon said airily; he bent and kissed his grandmother and smiled at Mia. 'Mia, the Contessa would be happy if you would lunch with her today. She is on the phone and I said I'd ask you.'

'Lunch with her—alone?' asked Mia, startled, her green eyes wide with amazament. 'But . . .'

Gideon grinned, 'I knew you'd be happy to lunch with her. Thanks, Mia.' He turned and walked away.

'But, Gideon—' Mia ran after him, clutching his arm, 'what will we talk about?'

He looked down at her with a smile. 'Don't worry, I told Annys that you were shy and needed help because of your father's death. You're the first person I've known Annys ask questions about, Mia. Normally she has no interest in anyone. As I told you the other day, I think you can help her.'

Mia let go of his arm and smoothed down her green overall. 'I'll try, Gideon, but . . .'

'Just try, Mia, that's all I ask of you,' he said, and went into his study, closing the door.

Mia saw that Gwyneth must have heard part of the talk, for she had obviously just come in from the garden. She was wearing cream shorts and a blue silk shirt, her black hair had a golden ribbon twisted in its braids, her eyes were bright with curiosity.

'What did Gideon ask of you?' she asked, half-laughing.

Mia stared at her for a moment and lifted her chin. 'As usual, he asked the impossible,' she said airily, and returned to the conservatory.

Madame le Bret looked at her with amusement. 'Now what's annoyed you? Gideon?'

Mia smiled, picking up some of the graceful white blooms, trying them in a flat green vase, standing back to admire them. 'Not Gideon this time,' she confessed. 'Gwyneth.'

A white carriage with two black horses came to fetch Mia for her luncheon date. She had wondered what to wear, remembering that Madame le Bret had said 'beautiful clothes are all that the Contessa has left to love.' In the end, Mia chose a dress she had bought in London against her better judgement, for it was unusual, a little dramatic, she had thought afterwards. Yet she loved the slender white dress with a slightly flared skirt. Made of very fine material, it was lined with silk, but the long sleeves were transparent. Mia studied her reflection carefully and hoped the frock looked all right.

Gideon was in the hall as she walked through it. He gave a soft whistle and when she looked at him, he smiled approval. 'A good choice, Mia. Annys will like that frock. If the conversation dies at any time, tell her you've heard she has some—what's the word you use?—fabulous?—some fabulous clothes. She loves them, spends hours, I understand, trying them on. That will get you over any gap.'

He flashed a quick smile at Mia, who said, 'Thanks, Gideon, I'm as scared as can be.'

Gideon looked at her, his eyes narrowed. 'Stop being scared, Mia, or Annys will sense it. She's just as frightened of you, don't forget. This is a big step for Annys to take. I think I'm the only other person on the island she has ever invited to the house. It's a beautiful house, full of treasures. You can also ask about them if the conversation drags.' He touched her hand lightly. 'You'll do fine, don't worry. Just be yourself.'

As the white carriage moved slowly along the winding road, Mia sat back and thought how much Gideon had changed. She hated having to admit it, but it was the truth—it was only since Gwyneth had arrived that Gideon had been so good-tempered, and stopped teasing her or being sarcastic.

Was it because he was so happy now Gwyneth was here? What could be the reason, otherwise? She turned before they went round a corner. Gideon was still standing outside the house, one hand lifted in farewell.

She caught her breath. She had never known love would be like this. This crazy mixed-up mass of emotions—longing to be

173

with him yet yearning to run away so that she could relax and not have to stand constant guard over her secret.

The house to which Mia was taken was built in Italian style, painted pastel rose, opening on to an inner courtyard, with fountains, and white statues, and urns full of orange and red flowers.

The Contessa came to greet her, wearing a white frock, trimmed with crimson poppies. She smiled at Mia and held out her hand.

'Please come in. What a charming frock. I see, that like me, you were discreet, choosing white so that our colours could not clash.'

The Contessa's eyes were still blank, Mia noticed; it was also an obvious effort for her to talk and smile, but as they sat in deep wicker chairs in the courtyard and drank long cool drinks, Mia found her nervousness leaving her.

'May I call you Mia? I don't know your surname,' the Contessa asked. 'Gideon is always talking about you and how happy you have made Madame le Bret.'

'Please do,' said Mia, dealing with the question first. 'Madame le Bret has been wonderfully kind.'

'I understand you came out because you lost your father, Mia. I am so sorry. I know what it is to lose a loved one.' The Contessa paused. 'You were very close? Your mother . . . ?'

Mia found it surprisingly easy to talk to this

beautiful unhappy woman who really showed an interest. Later, after lunch, Mia was shown the beautiful paintings, the exquisite glassware, the rich carpets, the silk curtains, but Annys showed it all with an impersonal air as if the beautiful things belonged to someone else. Her only warmth came to the surface when she showed Mia her huge wardrobe of clothes.

'As a diplomat's wife, I had to be always well and suitably dressed,' Annys explained. 'At first, it was a bore—then it became amusing—later, I turned it into a creative art. I see that you, also, have a good taste in clothes.'

'Thank you,' Mia said, and meant it. The gowns and furs were, as Gideon had said, fabulous.

Mia had a shock when the gilt French clock chimed four.

'Is it so late? I'm sorry . . . I mean, it's awfully . . . she stammered.

Annys smiled. 'Please, Mia. I too forgot the time. Madame le Bret will think I have eaten you.'

Mia stared at her. When the Contessa smiled, she was the most beautiful woman Mia had ever seen. Infinitely more beautiful than Gwyneth. Now Mia knew what Gideon had meant when he said he wished Mia had known the Contessa before tragedy struck.

'Please come again,' invited Annys as she saw Mia into the carriage.

Mia leaned forward. 'May I?' she asked. 'I have enjoyed it so much.'

The Contessa's pale cheeks were suddenly rosy. 'So have I,' she said warmly.

Gideon was waiting when Mia got home. He came to help her out, his face pleased. 'Good girl,' he said, and Mia knew that never had praise been so sweet. 'Annys just phoned to say what a pleasant time she had. It seems you two are *simpática*, as they say. You found plenty to talk about?'

'Plenty, thanks to your advice, Gideon, but we had very few blank spots. Her clothes are just too wonderful for words and she's so easy to talk to . . .'

The big man towering above her with his aquiline nose and sun-tanned face laughed. 'That's exactly what she said about you, Mia. She liked your dress?'

'Yes. She also wore white, but she's much more subtle, it was in order not to embarrass us if our colours clashed. I'd never have thought of that.'

'I very much doubt if the Contessa would have at your age, Mia,' said Gwyneth, strolling out from the house to join them. 'What sort of intellect has that woman got, Gideon, if she gets so excited about clothes?'

Mia caught her breath. 'The Contessa explained that as a diplomat's wife, it was her duty to be well dressed. She turned it into an art. It was probably as important to her husband to have a well-dressed wife as to have an intelligent one. Too much intelligence can, you know, become very boring,' said Mia, staring straight into Gwyneth's eyes.

Gideon choked on a cough and apologised. 'Care for a swim, Mia?'

Mia smiled. 'No, thanks, Gideon. Your grandmother will be longing to hear about the lunch so I'll go and see her.'

'Fine!'

'Let's go for a drive . . .' Gwyneth began. Then she laughed. 'I forgot, no cars, no drive. Let's take a walk along the beach, just for a change,' she said, a hint of mockery in her voice.

'All right,' agreed Gideon, and for the first time since she had met him, Mia thought he sounded tired.

*   *   *

On the day the cruising liner called in at the island, there was great excitement. The visits were rare and always appreciated by the little community who enjoyed their peaceful lives on the island, but also leapt at the chance to see a new face. Mia went down with several of Madame le Bret's friends to welcome the visitors. The residents would sort them out silently, and ask those they liked the look of to their houses to dine and drink. Mia only went because Madame le Bret said it would do her good—and because Gideon and Gwyneth had gone sailing.

Mia was glad to see Phoebe amongst the waiting crowd on the quay, and she slipped away from her elderly companions with a word of explanation, and joined the woman she believed to be her mother.

'Everyone's so thrilled, Phoebe!'

Phoebe turned and laughed. She was wearing a pale green linen suit and a rather shabby but gay hat. She looked much happier these days, Mia thought.

'It's always an occasion on the island. I usually come in case any of the people on board fall in love with the island and decide to stay and wait for the next boat. It happens quite often, you know, Mia . . . Mia!' she said again, but Mia was not listening.

She was staring at a short man with sandy hair who was waving to her from the ship's deck. His face was familiar, but . . . Now he was waving furiously with a big hanky.

'Mia!' he called. 'Don't you remember me? Toby . . . ?'

Toby! Her companion on the flight from Mombasa. Mia waved back.

'Hi, Toby!' she shouted.

'You know him?' Phoebe asked with a smile.

'We met on the plane coming out and Gideon was furious with me. Practically accused me of being disloyal to my fiancé because I talked to Toby,' Mia explained.

'It sounds like Gideon,' Phoebe laughed. 'No half-measures. What did you say?'

'I said being engaged didn't mean you couldn't speak to a man. After all, Phoebe, that would mean you couldn't be trusted.'

'Exactly—but somehow men don't seem to see it that way,' Phoebe said rather sadly.

At last the shouting and clapping and cheers died away, the gangplanks were down and the visitors pouring ashore.

Toby came running to take Mia's hands in his, swinging them as he smiled down at her. 'Gosh, it's good to see you, Mia,' he said.

Suddenly they were both laughing, Toby being introduced to Phoebe, Mia taking him, at Phoebe's suggestion, to one of the brightly painted carriages waiting for the tourists, and on a tour of the island.

Mia had forgotten what fun Toby was, how pleasant to talk to, and the hours flashed by. They stopped for lunch at an open-air restaurant under palm trees over-looking the ocean, and Toby told her of his good job in Victoria, on Mahé Island. He asked how she had got on, commented on the missing ring.

'Your engagement off?' he asked casually.

'Yes and no,' Mia told him. 'It is off, Toby, but no one here knows, and they mustn't know.'

'Why not?' he asked bluntly.

Mia hesitated, then she told him of Gideon and his advice.

'He's so horribly triumphant when he's proved right—which is most of the time,' she added ruefully. 'I know he'd congratulate me on having some sense at last.'

'He sounds utterly impossible,' said Toby, offering her a cigarette, leaning back in his chair relaxed.

'Oh, but he isn't,' Mia said quickly. 'Actually, Toby, I think it's my fault. I'm ridiculously sensitive where he's concerned.' She tried to laugh. 'Or that's what Phoebe and Madame le Bret say. Once Phoebe—she's the one you met at the dock—said I always lost my sense of humour when Gideon is near. He teases me a lot and I take it seriously. He will order people around, and most of them don't seem to mind . . .'

'But you obviously do,' Toby said, and laughed. 'This is a lovely place, Mia.' He looked round him. 'It's much quieter than Mahé, of course. Not that that's so very modern, but it's growing. My job . . .' He leaned forward to tell Mia about his work, and the time passed swiftly so that when the waiter came hovering round their table, and she saw they were the last customers, she suggested that Toby came home with her.

'Madame le Bret would love to meet you, I know,' she said.

The horse ambling along placidly, Toby and Mia went on talking happily, finding so much to say, so many shared interests. As they

180

reached the house, Mia turned to him.

'You won't forget that I'm still supposed to be engaged to Ian, will you?'

He squeezed her hand gently. 'I won't,' he promised.

As Mia had expected, Toby and Madame le Bret liked one another immediately and the old lady sent away the carriage at once.

'You are here for three days?' she asked Toby. '*C'est bon.* You will be our guest, please?'

Toby hesitated, looking at Mia, but she smiled and nodded.

'Yes, do, Toby, unless you have other plans.'

'I've no other plans. I only came to see—' he began, then stopped. 'I ought to go back and get my clothes,' he said worriedly.

'Do not deprive us of the joy of your company, Tobee,' said Madame le Bret with a warm smile, emphasising the last syllable of his name rather charmingly. 'It is a good thing that you have come at this time.'

Gideon and Gwyneth did not return for dinner, but Madame le Bret said there was no cause for alarm. 'Gideon has so many yachting friends who are sure to suggest dinner at the club, which Gwyneth enjoys.'

But every now and then through that evening, Mia did find herself worrying a little. Not much, for she knew that Gideon could cope with any emergency, handle any trouble, but on the long dark ride home, could Nero have stumbled, been lamed? she began to wonder.

Madame le Bret stayed up later than usual, encouraging Toby to talk, laughing at his way of putting things, thoroughly enjoying herself. When she finally left them, Mia and Toby walked down across the moon-swept lawn to the shadowy lagoon. The moon was full and bright, the palm trees silhouetted dramatically against the sky. The distant roar of the surf, the gentle sound of the lagoon was romantic, and she thought of Gideon and Gwyneth, sitting side by side in the carriage, probably Gideon's arm round Gwyneth's shoulder, her head on his chest . . .

'It's very beautiful, isn't it?' she said sharply, jumping up from the rock they were sitting on. 'Too beautiful sometimes. It makes me want to cry.'

'Does beauty always make you cry?' Toby asked.

'I don't know . . .' Mia fought to steady her voice and paused for a moment. She no longer knew anything about anyone.

How could she love and hate a man at the same time? How she could fear Gideon's anger—yet wasn't her fear merely because she wanted to impress him, to make him see her as a mature woman and not the teenager he always teasingly called her? Why did she hate him sometimes? Because he was arrogant and issued orders and she was no slave to jump to attention, she thought unhappily; yet at the same time she could not stop thinking about him.

Toby's three days with them passed swiftly and helped Mia ignore Gwyneth's possessiveness, which seemed to grow more pronounced every day. Oddly enough, Mia thought, Gideon did not like Toby—and Toby did not like Gwyneth.

'Sure, she's beautiful, if you like that artificial stuff,' Toby said bluntly when Mia talked of Gwyneth. 'But she's hard as nails. I wouldn't like her to have designs on me.' He gave an exaggerated shudder which dissolved them both in laughter.

It seemed to Mia that with Toby, they hardly ever stopped laughing. Gideon would sit silently, his face grim, his eyes disapproving as he watched them.

'Anyone would think he was my guardian,' Mia said angrily to Toby.

Toby chuckled. 'Don't forget he thinks you're still engaged.'

Mia's hand flew to her mouth. 'I'd forgotten,' she confessed.

Yet, when she came to think about it in bed that night as she tossed restlessly in the heat, what difference did that make? She and Toby were simply good friends, no more. Even if she had still been engaged to Ian, she could still have laughed with Toby. But should she have? Mia wondered that last night, as she walked

183

barefoot with Toby along the warmly damp sand, hand in hand, looking at the mountain that towered over them, while the perfume of a million flowers seemed to drift towards them.

'Mia,' Toby said abruptly, stopping, turning her to face him, 'I've been trying not to say this, for I know it's pretty soon after . . . Well, what I mean is I didn't mean to rush things, but . . .' His hands on her shoulders, he looked into her eyes.

'Mia, I love you,' he said simply. 'Is there any hope?'

'Oh, Toby,' she said in real dismay, 'I like you so much, but . . .'

He let go of her and she saw the look in his eyes.

'I am so sorry, Toby,' she went on. 'I thought you had a girlfriend.'

He shook his head. 'I said that on the plane to make things right. I knew you'd be more relaxed with me if you thought I was what my gran would call "bespoke." '

He tried to smile, dug his hands deep in his trouser pockets and they began to walk again, slowly, their feet sinking into the wet sand as the tiny waves crept in over their toes. 'I should have known,' he went on, kicking at a small shell.

'Should have known what?' Mia asked, looking at him worriedly. Was it her fault? Should she have been less friendly?

He stopped again to look at her. 'It's Gideon, isn't it?'

She could have denied it a thousand times, but her red, hot face would have betrayed her, she knew.

'Is it so obvious?' she asked at once.

He smiled. 'Only to someone who loves you, Mia.'

'He mustn't know—ever,' said Mia.

'Why not? Surely he's the one who should know?'

Mia twisted her hands together. 'But don't you see, I—I mean nothing to him. He thinks I'm young and—naive and—besides, everyone here thinks he loves the Contessa, and Gwyneth thinks—'

'She thinks what she wants to think,' Toby said grimly. 'It's what's known as positive thinking. Maybe you should try some.'

Mia tried to laugh. 'It would be just a waste of time.'

They walked back towards the house slowly, Mia trying to think of something to say to comfort Toby. Just below the terrace, which was, she saw, in darkness, only the soft glow from the hall light showing, which meant that Gideon had gone to bed, she stopped Toby. She looked up at him unhappily, a shaft of moonlight falling across her face, giving it a strangely ethereal look, a look of youth and innocence, a look of compassion.

'I'm so sorry, Toby, if it was my fault. I like

you so much.'

He smiled, bent down and kissed her gently. 'It wasn't your fault, Mia, so don't worry. It's just one of those things. I'll never forget you, ever, and if—if at any time you change your mind or you need help, promise you'll get in touch with me?' He lifted her hand and held it against his cheek. 'I'd do anything for you, Mia, anything,' he said softly.

'I promise, Toby,' Mia said urgently.

The light on the terrace suddenly blazed and Mia and Toby looked up. Gideon was standing there, impressive in a richly scarlet dressing-gown.

'It's late,' Gideon said flatly.

'Yes—too late,' Toby said with a wry smile. 'Good-night, Mia. Thanks for everything.'

'I'll see you in the morning—' Mia began.

Toby smiled. 'I'll be off early. We're sailing at eight o'clock.'

'I've already told Pen to have the carriage here in good time,' Gideon said curtly.

Toby looked at him. For a moment Mia was afraid. It was like two dogs sparring before a fight—assessing one another, their hackles raised.

Then Toby smiled. 'Thanks—for every-thing,' he said, and turned and walked into the house.

Mia went up the steps to stand by Gideon. Her heart was beating furiously, she was so angry she could hardly speak. 'Is it necessary to be so rude to my friends?' she asked, her voice unsteady.

Gideon opened the door wider and stood back. 'We'll discuss that tomorrow when you're in a more reasonable mood,' he said curtly. 'Goodnight.'

She was not surprised in the morning when, as she sat talking to Madame le Bret, both bemoaning the fact of Toby's departure, the message came from Gideon that he wished to see her at once.

At once! she thought angrily. She had a very good mind to tell him she would see him when it was convenient to her and not before. She was so heartily sick of his rudeness, she thought angrily, as she walked to the study.

'Come in,' he said curtly in answer to her knock. She went in and he was standing by the window, his back turned. 'Well?' he said.

'You wanted to see me?' she said, a little disconcerted by the strange greeting.

He swung round. 'I did not *want* to see you,' he said, 'but I felt I must. There is quite a difference,' he added, his voice cold. 'You stand there looking so innocent and hurt, wondering what I have to say to you. Have you no loyalty? No love for the man you're engaged to?'

Mia closed her eyes for a second, unaware of the shadows her long lashes made on her fine skin. Who was it wrote something about a web you weave when first you practise to

187

deceive? How right Toby was—it was Ian Gideon was thinking of.

'I have not forgotten,' Mia said with equal coldness. How could she ever forget it if she had been engaged to a man like Gideon?

Ian had written her two letters already, begging her to change her mind, asking for details of what she knew about her real parents so that he could help look for them. Obviously he was afraid that the knowledge that Mia was not the child of the Bartons would disturb his parents, and might make them put pressure on him to break the engagement himself. Mia had written back, gently but firmly, telling him that she no longer loved him, that it was better to know now than later, and that she was very, very sorry.

Now she wished she had told Gideon the truth. She was tempted to tell him right there and then, but it would only anger him more, make him accuse her of lying to him, which she had done, and make the whole situation worse. When he and Gwyneth went back to London, Mia decided, she would write and tell Gideon she had broken off the engagement. Gideon's sarcasm would not hurt so much on paper.

'Flirting with Toby like some infatuated adolescent,' Gideon was saying angrily. 'I've never seen such flagrant behaviour, leading him on as you did. I suppose he thought as you weren't wearing a ring that you were free.'

Mia lifted her small pointed chin and

looked Gideon in the eyes. 'He knew about my engagement,' she said, and that at least was the truth. 'Nor were we flirting. We were good friends, that's all.'

'So good friends kiss in the moonlight, do they?' Gideon asked, his voice rich with the sarcasm she hated.

Her cheeks suddenly warm, Mia again told the truth. 'He had just said he loved me and wished I could marry him, so . . . so I—I was sorry for him and let him kiss me. It meant nothing.'

'It meant nothing to you, perhaps,' Gideon's voice cut like a sharp knife. 'But I saw his face.'

Suddenly Mia's lower lip trembled. Poor Toby! Was it her fault, then? But she had not known he was going to kiss her, or that he would fall in love with her when they had known one another for so short a time, she thought.

Fortunately for her self-control, Gideon went on speaking, and his next words made her so angry that the desire to cry vanished.

'D'you let every man who proposes to you kiss you?' Gideon demanded, standing by her, his mouth a thin line. 'If I proposed to you, would you let me kiss you?'

She tilted her head to glare up at him. 'I most certainly would not.'

'Why not?'

'Because—because you wouldn't mean it,'

Mia told him angrily. 'You'd just say it for—for—' she paused. 'Toby meant every word he said, so—so—'

'How would you know I didn't mean it?' Gideon asked.

'Because—because—'

Suddenly and unexpectedly she was in his arms. He was holding her close, his arms hard and tight round her. Now he lifted one arm, using his hand to tilt back her chin, holding her firmly so that she could not escape if she tried. Not that she did try . . .

She stood very still, feeling the hard thumping of her heart, shivering a little as his warm hand touched her chin, and then closing her eyes as his mouth came down on hers.

Hard. Almost fiercely.

He held her so tightly that she almost cried out with pain, but for a moment everything seemed to spin round her, stars, tiny moons, little suns whirled as his mouth met hers.

The door opened and Gideon straightened, letting go of Mia abruptly, so that she nearly fell and had to clutch at a chair.

Gwyneth stood in the doorway, her face amused. She was obviously waiting to go swimming, as she wore a loose white towelling coat over her black bikini.

'Really, Gideon,' she said teasingly, 'isn't there a law against kissing minors? Surely Mia's had enough with her adoring Toby hanging around.'

Mia had got her balance, she gave Gideon one quick look and then slipped past Gwyneth, who stood there, smiling as if it was one huge joke.

CHAPTER NINE

The plane flew in the following day and Mia met Walter King, the young executive Gideon had mentioned to her; a tall, thin, smart man, he was so exactly the person Ian Yates's father wanted Ian to be and that, no matter how hard Ian tried, he could never succeed in being, that she was not sure whether to laugh or cry.

The information Walter King brought, however, was serious enough to make Gideon decide to end his holiday immediately.

'Don't fret, Grand'mère,' he said to Madame le Bret, who looked stricken at the news, 'I'll be back for the children.' He looked across the room at Mia. 'D'you want a lift back to Mombasa yet?'

'Oh no!' Madame le Bret cried, and then put her lace-edged hanky to her mouth and tried to smile at Mia. 'You must go when you wish to, dear child.'

'No, I don't want to go back yet,' Mia said firmly, meeting Gideon's eyes and knowing what he was thinking.

Gwyneth asked Mia to help her pack, much

to Mia's surprise, but when she was alone with Gwyneth, Mia knew that the request had been merely an excuse to get her alone.

Gwyneth came to the point quickly. 'Mia, I think for your own good you should know something.'

Mia's mouth twisted wryly. She had heard this sort of remark so often before from different people, and it was always the prelude to something unpleasant. She turned and looked at Gwyneth. 'Should I?' she asked.

Gwyneth was wearing blue slacks and a yellow blouse, a combination that might not have suited everyone, but with her dark hair brushed back, she looked more beautiful than ever. Now her face was grave, but she spoke cautiously.

'I know you'll hate me for saying this, Mia, but you are very young and vulnerable. You're engaged to one man, yet you could flirt with Toby, and I've often seen you look at Gideon as if . . .'

Mia clenched her hands and made herself smile. 'As if?'

Gwyneth sat on the edge of the bed and frowned. 'This isn't a joke, Mia. I just want you to know that Gideon and I have an understanding.'

Mia smiled blandly—at least, she hoped it was a bland smile, if that was the right expression. 'You have?'

'Yes, we have,' Gwyneth said curtly,

obviously getting annoyed. 'We're going to be married.' She paused.

Mia showed no surprise. 'When?'

Gwyneth frowned. 'We haven't arranged the details yet—I know Gideon would want to be married out here so that his grandmother could be there, but . . .'

Mia smiled sweetly. 'Wouldn't you like it?'

Gwyneth fidgeted. 'I hate this place. Parochial, provincial . . .'

'Pretty.' Mia supplied the word with another smile.

Gwyneth stood up and went to the mirror, pretending to look at her reflection, but Mia could see that she was actually watching her. 'Gideon has said several times that he finds your—your interest in him, shall we say, very embarrassing. After all, he's been most generous to you. Paying your fare out here . . .'

Mia's cheeks flamed. 'I've spoken to him about it. He said I must ask you for the account.'

Gwyneth turned and smiled, her eyes hard. 'But you haven't asked me, Mia. See what I mean? If I hadn't mentioned it, you probably wouldn't have and I know he would never have said anything to me. In addition you have been staying here without, I imagine, paying for your board, so you've had a pleasant cheap holiday. Why not call it a day and go home to the man you're going to marry?'

Mia crossed her legs and looked at the blue

Indian Ocean. 'Because I'm not ready to go yet.'

'Will you ever be ready?' Gwyneth asked. 'It's not fair on Ian.'

'Ian knows why I'm staying here.'

'But does he know the real reason?'

Mia turned and this time could smile naturally. 'He does.'

Gwyneth looked taken aback, but she went on, 'You see, it could be embarrassing for everyone when we come out again to be married, if you're here and—'

Mia stood up. 'I can't imagine Gideon being embarrassed by anything, but I promise you one thing, I won't be here to dance at your wedding.'

'You won't?'

'No,' Mia said firmly. 'For the simple reason that I don't believe he's going to marry you.' Suddenly she knew that was the truth. Gwyneth had betrayed her own uncertainty by the way she had spoken. Had Gideon told Gwyneth he loved her, she would not have needed to try to frighten Mia.

Gwyneth looked so startled that Mia found it hard not to laugh. 'You don't? But I've just told you—'

'You've just told me what you believe is going to happen. I'll believe it when Gideon tells me. All of us here on this island believe Gideon will marry the Contessa.'

'The Contessa?' Gwyneth echoed. 'But he

194

hardly ever sees her. I mean, he's not often here, and she looks so vacant and lost—'

'Not when she laughs,' said Mia. 'She's changed a lot even since I've been here. She is the most beautiful woman I've ever seen in my life.'

Gwyneth was obviously thinking hard. 'When I'm not here, does Gideon spend a lot of time with her?'

'He dines with her several times a week,' Mia told her, and added, 'Alone.'

'I never realised that,' Gwyneth said slowly. 'She writes to him, I know. The letters come marked Personal, but I recognise the postmark and also her big flowing handwriting. Besides, she always uses green ink—another example of her desire to make people aware of her.' Gwyneth stood up. 'Mia, thanks for telling me about the Contessa. Thanks a lot,' she added as Mia walked out of the room.

Mia felt rather ashamed of her own cattiness as she hurried back to Madame le Bret, yet wasn't it the truth? Mia felt more sure than ever that Gwyneth had invented the story about having an 'understanding' with Gideon just to warn her off. She suddenly thought of something with dismay. Maybe she had done the wrong thing, for perhaps knowing about the Contessa would make Gwyneth come out here with Gideon every time, and Madame le Bret would not be too pleased about that.

195

The day Gideon and Gwyneth left the island, Mia thought how odd it was, although she hated the idea of his going, yet at the same time she longed to get it over. Now she must hurry up her search for her mother.

The days passed swiftly. Regularly Mia went to see Phoebe, but her questions got her no further. Phoebe was evasive about what she had done before she met and married Reg; she said little more about her parents except repeating that she had been expected to do what she was told!

Mia acquired the habit of going to visit the Contessa every afternoon while Madame le Brett took her siesta. The white carriage with the two black horses would be waiting outside the house and Mia would be whisked off to the Italian chalet.

More and more as she grew to know the Contessa better now—she had to call her Annys—Mia felt relaxed. Sometimes they talked about the past, but not often. Annys never talked about her parents and only said once casually that she had gone to finishing school in Switzerland, and had added, with a rueful smile, that she had never properly 'finished' there.

'I ran away,' she said, and changed the subject.

There were days when Annys would talk about her life as a diplomat's wife, making Mia laugh. Once Annys said sadly that she had not

196

loved her husband when she married him, but with each year that had passed, she had learned to love him more. Annys never mentioned the child she had longed for and who had died so tragically. Often Mia felt tempted to confide in Annys, and tell her about her search for her mother, but something always stopped her. Suppose—though to Mia it was not even remotely likely—Annys proved to be her missing mother? Mia thought. Would that be the cure for Annys's sadness? Or would it only intensify her feeling of guilt?

Madame le Bret began to plan for the annual week's holiday she gave for the orphans, and Mia found herself caught up in the organising. The frail old lady's cheeks glowed and her eyes shone brightly as they discussed every aspect of the visit—or what Pen called rather dourly 'the onslaught,' and Mia without thinking said one day :

'You're a wasted grandmother, Madame le Bret. You should have had a dozen grandchildren.'

The old lady smiled sadly. 'I had hoped for a dozen great-grandchildren, but Gideon takes so long to make up his mind. He is nearly thirty-four and still single.'

'Perhaps he'll marry a widow with a dozen children,' Mia joked, trying to make the old lady more cheerful.

Madame le Bret shook her head. 'That I

cannot imagine, Mia. Gideon is good with children and, with his own, would be a perfect father, but other people's children? I don't think it would work. He would be kind, tolerant, perhaps more tolerant than with his own children, but it would not be the same.'

'Reg Haseldine says he could never tolerate another man's child,' said Mia.

'I can understand that, since his accident,' Madame le Bret admitted. 'But it is hard on Phoebe. She should have several children, there is so much love in her.'

'Isn't there?' Mia agreed warmly.

Gideon arrived the day after the children arrived. It had been like a mixture of a nightmare and fun, Mia was not sure which! The ship had docked and the children, ranging from four years of age to twelve or thirteen, had swarmed ashore, climbing with excited shouts into the horse-bus that awaited them. As usual, for according to Pen it always happened, there were more children than they had expected, but as the nun, her serene face beautiful in the framework of the white coif, said with an apologetic smile to Madame le Bret :

'You made them so happy before—it is difficult to refuse.'

'I don't know if I'm growing smaller or older, or my eyes are not good,' said Madame le Bret, looking over the wall of the terrace down to where the children were racing round

198

the beach, shouting and laughing, 'but two or three of the boys look older than twelve to me.'

Mother Catherine blushed. 'I am the one at fault, Madame le Bret. They have been good boys all the year and they came to me and said, can't we go once more? Just once more? I knew you would not say no.'

When Gideon arrived, he changed and went straight down to the beach, and Mia was surprised to hear the cries of glee as the children hurled themselves at him. He was wearing white shorts over his swimming trunks and he walked along the sand with several children clinging to him, one on his back, one round his neck, the others dangling from his arms.

'I never realised he loved children,' Mia said to Madame le Bret, who had wheeled her chair down the smooth lawn to where she could sit in the shade, and watch the children making sand castles and rushing joyfully into the lagoon.

Madame le Bret gave her an odd look. 'There are a lot of things about Gideon that you do not realise, my child.'

Halfway through lunch, the butler came in and spoke softly in Gideon's ear. Gideon frowned and stood up at once, his chair nearly falling over with the abruptness of his movement.

'If you will excuse me, Grand'mère,' he said.

She looked worried. 'Bad news?'

He smiled. 'No—probably a mountain made out of a molehill, but I'd better get it settled.'

Mia was in the Contessa's white carriage when she saw the doctor's carriage going towards Le Bret Manor. She wondered if Madame le Bret was ill and had not told her, so as not to spoil Mia's afternoon.

When Mia returned just before tea, she heard crying. The children were gathered in groups on the lawn before the house, some sobbing bitterly. Mia went down to ask the nun in charge what was wrong.

Sister Mary was young and her eyes were bewildered. 'I don't know,' she admitted. 'We have just been told by Mr. Eastwood that the outing tomorrow is off. We are confined to the grounds and must not go outside them.'

'Mr. Eastwood said that?' Mia was puzzled. 'But why? At lunchtime we were discussing it all and he said nothing.'

As if in sympathy with the children's tears, the sky had clouded over and the sun vanished. Everything looked different, Mia thought. There was an ominous stillness in the air, the lagoon had lost its bright colour, there were great shadows stretching everywhere.

'Perhaps there is some mistake . . .'

Sister Mary shrugged. 'I am wondering if it is a punishment. Mr. Eastwood found the three older boys playing on the roof without shoes—you know that is forbidden—and also without supervision, and he was very angry.'

'Was that at lunchtime?' Mia asked.

The young nun shrugged her shoulders. 'I do not know when it was. I only know that Mother Catherine called the boys to her and was sad because they were disobedient, for she had trusted them.'

'Perhaps I can find out what's happened,' offered Mia.

Sister Mary smiled ruefully. 'It would be good if you can, for the children long for this outing, it is so different from their life at the orphanage.'

When she saw Gideon walking from the tents, she hurried to meet him. 'Gideon, is it true the outing is off?'

He was frowning. 'Yes,' he said curtly. He was wearing khaki shorts and a jacket and looked heartbreakingly handsome, Mia thought.

'Why?'

Gideon stood still, almost as still, Mia thought, as the trees behind him. There was an oppressive stillness in the air.

'Because I said so,' he said.

'But they look forward to it so much,' said Mia. 'Gideon, it's not fair to punish them all if one or two are naughty. They are so young and this is such a wonderful holiday for them . . .' The words tumbled eagerly out of her mouth as she stared up at him pleadingly. 'Couldn't you just punish the ones concerned?'

Gideon's smile was a strange one. There was no humour in it, only a kind of ruefulness. 'D'you think that's why I've cancelled the outing? Because a couple of the kids were naughty? Honestly, Mia, sometimes you amaze me. What sort of man d'you think I am?'

Mia hesitated. 'That's what I understood from Sister Mary . . .'

'Sister Mary is very young and has no idea what she's talking about,' said Gideon, walking past her. 'You should be good friends, you're so alike.'

Mia stood, staring at his back as he walked up to the house. She turned away blindly. Why must Gideon always put a sting in his remarks? she wondered. Why keep reminding her that she was 'very young'?

Why, she thought, as she walked down to the lagoon and stood tossing shells into the water carelessly, why must she fall in love with such a man? A man who could only hurt her.

It was at breakfast next morning that Mother Catherine arrived, a little breathless, her usually serene face concerned, her dark blue eyes worried. 'Mr. Eastwood,' she began, walking from the terrace into the breakfast room.

Gideon, who had been standing by the sideboard, helping himself from the warming-stand, turned, his eyes alert.

'A fresh case?' he asked. He pulled out a chair. 'A cup of coffee, Mother Catherine, to help you relax?' he said with a quick smile, gesturing to Mia to pour one out.

Mia obeyed quickly. Why was the Mother Superior looking so frightened?

'It's those boys, Mr. Eastwood,' the elderly nun said sadly. 'They have run away.'

Gideon smiled and Mia thought he looked relieved. He was wearing a thin grey suit and had told Mia he had to go to the shipping yard on urgent business and was in a hurry, but now, as he sat down by the Mother Superior's side, he seemed relaxed and patient.

'Boys will be boys, Mother Superior. They'll return.' She twisted her long fingers together. 'I do not think so, Mr. Eastwood. They confided in one who was too young to climb—they said they were going to climb the mountain.'

'When did they leave?' Gideon asked.

'I am not sure—I think it was as dawn broke.'

'You've only just discovered it?'

She nodded. 'We have roll-call after breakfast on holiday and they were missing. I talked to the children, and little Louis wept and said they had gone. One of them is his brother, and I think he's afraid for him.'

Gideon stood up. 'Don't worry. I'll organise a search party at once. Has Louis any idea which way they went?'

'No—only that they said it would be easier to climb the rocks above the lagoon and it would be a short cut.'

'Mia, look after Mother Superior,' Gideon said curtly. 'And help organise some games to keep the children happy. It's bad enough without this.'

The elderly nun rose. 'No, no, Mia my child, I do not need help. It is better that you, knowing the island well, should help in the search.'

Gideon hesitated, then nodded. 'All right, come with me, Mia. I'll get you to phone some of my men while I'm organising a search party from here.'

Soon the search party was on its way. Gideon said he thought the boys might have told the young brother wrong directions to throw the search party—which they must have known would look for them—off the right track.

'You're not angry with them?' queried Mia, surprised.

Gideon looked at her. 'My dear Mia, you may find it hard to believe, but I was a boy once. I too ran away from school. I know why they did it—because they're mad with me. Like you, they think I'm punishing the whole lot of them because these three boys were naughty.'

'That isn't the reason?'

His eyes were cold. 'No, it most certainly is not.'

She had to stay by the phone in case any

news came in from the different search parties. As the morning passed and the great clouds in the sky thickened even more threateningly, the tension grew.

Madame le Bret wheeled her chair to Mia's side. 'There is a bad storm coming,' she said worriedly. 'If those children are caught in it—'

It was in the middle of the afternoon—Mia having sent the Contessa's carriage back with an apologetic explanatory letter—when Gideon walked into the house. Madame le Bret had forgone her siesta; she was too worried to sleep, she had said.

'The storm's getting nearer,' Gideon said curtly. 'I'm taking up the helicopter. Like to come, Mia?'

'Why . . .' Mia began, standing up.

'The helicopter—in the storm?' Madame le Bret asked worriedly.

Gideon bent to kiss her. 'Grand'mère, it is nothing to worry about. We shall be back long before the storm breaks, but the search parties can find no trace. We may see them from the air. They may be hurt—that's why I need Mia. She's good with children.'

Absurdly pleased by his confidence in her, Mia hurriedly changed into dark blue jeans, a white blouse and a thick chunky white sweater, for Gideon had said that, if the storm broke, it could turn very cold.

It was the first time she had ever been up in a helicopter, and Mia's heart gave a little frightened jump as the machine rose up in the air, its fan-like propellor whirling noisily, the helicopter itself lurching drunkenly as it sought the right height.

'They're wearing white shirts,' Gideon said curtly, 'so keep your eyes open. Also for a plume of smoke. If they're lost or hurt, they may signal.'

Mia kept her eyes fixed on the ground below, searching through the thick trees, the spreading bush, the huge grotesquely carved rocks. Soon they were near the mountain, circling it when suddenly the helicopter tipped sideways.

'Hang on!' Gideon shouted, and Mia obeyed.

It was a nightmare few minutes, seeming like hours to Mia, as the helicopter straightened and lurched and suddenly began to drop.

'Got to land,' Gideon shouted. 'Don't panic!' Mia did what she always did when frightened; she didn't panic, she prayed instead.

There was quite a vicious bump as the helicopter landed on the side of the mountain and she was jerked violently, banging her head so that everything spun round and went black.

When she opened her eyes, the rain was beating down on her. She was in Gideon's arms, her face turned against his chest as he walked as fast as he could along the uneven, narrow path round the mountain. There was a terrific noise, like the wailing of a hundred banshees, she thought, and the heavy fall of rain stung her face like needles.

She must have stirred, for Gideon spoke.

'Everything's under control, Mia; just keep still,' he said cheerfully.

'What—happened?'

'The storm came before I expected it—we got caught up in the wind and I had to land. You must have hit your head or fainted.'

'Where—where are we going?'

'I'm trying to find a cave—somewhere to get out of this darned wind and rain.' He was walking sideways now, slowly, and Mia opened her eyes again and saw that far below them was a deep drop into a ravine.

'I could walk, Gideon . . .'

'Just keep still and do what you're told,' he said curtly.

She obeyed, for the slightest movement, she knew, could throw them both down the side of the mountain.

It seemed hours before Gideon turned and could walk more quickly, but now they were in full range of the wind that howled and tore at them. She shivered.

'Cold?' he asked. 'Good thing you wore that jersey. Once we're out of the wind it won't be so bad.'

At last he found a cave—if it could be dignified by such a name. It was more of a recess in the rocks, but with a big overhanging ledge above affording some shelter from the wind and rain. Gideon put her down gently, keeping his arm round her for a moment as the world swayed around her.

'It's a funny feeling,' she said, and tried to laugh.

He helped her sit down as far back from the opening as possible, then pulled a flask from his pocket and gave her a small drink. The brandy burned her throat and made her cough, but it warmed and steadied her.

'Thank you,' she said, 'I'm sorry I . . . I fainted. Something hit me . . .' She rubbed her hand over the back of her head gingerly. 'Oh, it's sore there!'

It was dark in the cave, but outside they could see the torrential rain falling like a grey curtain and every now and then heard a crashing sound.

'I'm sorry for those kids,' said Gideon, looking out of the cave into the half-light. 'I only hope they've found a cave like this.'

'What about the tents?' Mia asked, suddenly remembering the children.

'They should be all right. We're usually sheltered at the house, just round the corner and protected from most of the winds. Pen will cope. He's an old hand at handling storms. Probably house all the kids indoors. I'm more worried about my grandmother when we don't get home.'

Mia caught her breath. 'Yes, she'll think we've—we've crashed. Gideon, was it—was she the one the doctor came to see yesterday? I saw him coming up as I went to visit Annys. Only—only your grandmother said nothing to me, and I was worried.'

There was a little pause—it seemed suddenly quiet, for they had been shouting at one another in order to be heard above the wailing roar of the wind and rain.

'You're very fond of her, aren't you?' Gideon said slowly.

'Very, very fond,' Mia agreed.

'She's going to miss you,' he shouted.

It was as if something inside her lurched. She always dreaded the thought of leaving the island, for she had no idea where she could go. She shivered, and Gideon moved to her side, taking off his wool-lined jacket and wrapping it round her, holding his arm round her as he shouted: 'Scared?'

She shook her head as the wind whirled and beat against the rocks round them. A terrific crash made her shiver again and his arm tightened round her.

'It sounds worse than it is!' he yelled.

'Isn't there anything we can do?' Mia shouted.

'Not a thing till it stops,' he yelled back.

The rain never let up for a second. It was exactly like a thick grey curtain cutting off the outside world and as the brief twilight came and went and darkness fell, Gideon sat near to Mia, leaning against the rock. She took off his coat.

'I'm warm now, thanks,' she yelled. 'You'll freeze!'

He put on the coat and made the knapsack into a pillow for her. 'Try to sleep and it'll soon be over,' he yelled in turn.

When she awoke, the sun was shining. She was lying on the ground, covered by Gideon's coat. She sat up and the pain made her cry out. She touched her head gingerly and stared at her hand. It looked as if the wound had started to bleed again.

Struggling to her feet, she went outside and stopped dead, for the cave led to a narrow ledge with a deep fall into the shaded ravine below. She hesitated. Where was Gideon? Was he all right? He might have gone to find a way down the mountainside, she thought, and if she wasn't here, when he came back . . .

She felt stiff and sore, her head throbbed, and suddenly Gideon walked along the narrow ledge as casually as if it had been a wide pavement.

'I've sent up a signal. We can get up higher along here and make our way down to one of the paths. They'll be able to meet us. How d'you feel?'

'A bit giddy and—a bit stiff,' Mia told him.

He took her into the cave and examined her head. 'You've got a nasty cut, but nothing serious,' he told her.

'How did you signal?'

He laughed. 'I couldn't find anything dry, so I burned my shirt. I saw an answering smoke from the valley, so I know I was seen.'

Mia saw then that his blue jersey was all he wore with his khaki trousers.

'I think I can walk . . .' she said carefully.

'Good, we'll take it slowly.' He put his hands on her shoulders and looked down at her. 'Promise you'll tell me the instant you feel giddy or tired?' He paused while she nodded. 'You were a good girl last night, Mia,' he went on. 'It must have been a nightmare.'

Looking into his grey eyes, suddenly so close, she was tempted to tell him the truth. That it would have been a nightmare if he had not been with her—that she could bear anything bravely if only he was there.

Instead, she smiled. 'It wasn't a picnic!'

He laughed as they edged their way along the narrow path, Mia leading the way with Gideon holding her hand. The path circled and climbed and several times they had to pause, as giddiness swept over Mia. But each time Gideon's arm went round her and he pressed her face against his chest until the world was steady again.

It was a long but easy climb down the less steep side of the mountain to the valley, but Mia was glad when they reached the path that led through the trees, for her head was

211

throbbing badly. Perhaps Gideon saw the strain on her face, for he said nothing but simply lifted her off the ground and carried her.

Vaguely Mia heard shouts, and suddenly the search party met them. Mia was half asleep as they made a stretcher very primitively but effectively and she was made to lie down on it. The gentle swaying movement lulled her to sleep, and the next thing she knew was being back at the house, with Madame le Bret openly weeping with relief and the doctor suddenly there.

He must have given Mia an injection, for she knew nothing more, and when she awoke, the sun was streaming into her bedroom and there was a bandage round her head. She looked round and Madame le Bret wheeled her chair forward and held Mia's hand.

'My poor child . . . and how do you feel?'

Mia smiled. 'Sleepy—drugged—but my headache's better.' She sat up too quickly and the world spun for a second. Then she tried again more gingerly. 'Are the boys all right?'

Madame le Bret seemed to have aged overnight; her face was tired and peaked, her eyes sad. 'Yes—they had not gone away. They were hiding and laughing because of the excitement they had caused. Their idea of a joke!'

'Oh no!' Mia cried out in amazement. 'Why, the young . . .'

'They have been punished enough,' Madame le Bret said wisely. 'When you and Gideon were missing I think they learned a lesson.'

'And Gideon?'

'He is at the shipping yard. There is trouble there. The manager is very sick,' Madame le Bret said worriedly, then she smiled. 'But there is also good news—that you and Gideon are safe. Was it very terrifying?'

'It would have been—without Gideon,' Mia confessed.

Madame le Bret smiled. 'Ah, he is a good man to be with you when you are in trouble. But now, the doctor said, you must sleep.'

Mia caught the hand resting on hers. 'Madame le Bret, you are all right? I thought I saw the doctor come to see you yesterday, or was it the day before?'

'It was not for me he came. Several of the children are sick—colds, I think. Nothing serious.'

'Oh, good,' Mia said with relief. 'Now I'll sleep.'

She woke just before it was dinner time. She felt much better, got up, washed and carefully dressed in a green frock. This time she was not afraid of Gideon. It seemed as if she had met a new Gideon during the time they had sheltered from the storm, a kind, under-standing man—no longer the sarcastic and often cruel Gideon she hated, or had hated.

Gideon came to join them after dinner. He had showered and changed into his evening clothes. He stood in the doorway, tall, broad-shouldered, incredibly handsome in the formal clothes with the red cummerbund round his waist.

'Feeling better?' he asked Mia, but did not wait for an answer. Instead he went to Mother Superior and took her hand in his.

'Good news, Mother,' he said, his voice gentle. 'I have just seen the doctor. It is a perfectly harmless ailment and not the typhoid we feared.'

'Oh, thank the Good God for that,' said Mother Superior, her face bright.

'Typhoid?' Madame le Bret repeated sharply.

Gideon turned to her. 'The doctor was afraid two of the children had it. He had to take certain tests before he could be certain it was not typhoid. That's why I cancelled the outing, as it meant quarantine for them all until we were sure.'

There was a little stillness. 'Why—why didn't you tell us?' asked Mia.

Gideon looked at her, his grey eyes cold. 'Because people are apt to panic. Typhoid on this island could have caused nasty repercussions. That's why I had to take drastic measures to ensure that the disease was not spread.'

'But I thought . . .' Mia began.

'You thought I did it to punish them all for what a couple of boys had done?' Gideon said for her. His voice was cold and unfriendly, his grey eyes hostile, she saw with dismay.

'I'm sorry, Gideon,' she apologised.

He looked at her. 'It's a little late, Mia. You made it plain the sort of man you think I am,' he said, and turned to his grandmother.

Mia sat very still. She felt as if he had hit her in the face. Perhaps the Mother Superior had seen the shock in Mia's eyes, for she moved to sit by her side, talking of the children, covering up Mia's long silence so that no one need notice.

CHAPTER TEN

As the children's visit to the island drew towards the end, Phoebe had a wonderful idea.

'We'll give a big birthday party for them all and bake just as many iced cakes as we can manage,' she said eagerly, 'so that they all can eat just as much as they like for once.'

Madame le Bret, who had been looking old and tired since the day of the storm and Gideon and Mia's ordeal, looked interested.

'I have an even better idea, Phoebe, my child.' She lifted her frail hand. '*Ecoutez, s'il vous plait*,' she said with sudden gaiety, 'this is my plan.'

215

Phoebe, Mia, and several of the old lady's friends who had come to dine with her listened obediently.

'Let us make it a competition,' Madame le Bret went on. 'We will auction the cakes. The gentlemen will buy the cake and his partner for the evening. No one will know for whose cake he has bid,' she laughed. 'We will hold a dance, and the beautiful lady who baked the cake the lucky man bought must dance with him all the time.'

Amidst general laughter, Phoebe approved of the plan. 'But where did you hear of it?'

Madame le Bret shrugged. 'I read about it— it is, I think, an American custom,' she smiled. 'The money we raise we will spend on the children for toys and clothes. Phoebe, you will organise it, yes?'

Phoebe agreed—for apparently she organised most things. Everyone seemed interested and promised to help; even Annys Severini agreed to bake and ice a cake when Mia told her.

Annys was looking even more beautiful than ever, Mia thought, as she watched the slender graceful woman in her white slacks and vivid scarlet shirt.

'Mia, I've surprised you?' Annys said, and laughed. She leaned forward and patted Mia's hand. 'You've done me a lot of good. Gideon asked me to help you get over the loss of your father, but you've helped me far more than I

216

could ever help you.'

They were in the courtyard, basking in the sunshine.

'You have helped me,' Mia said quickly. She was wearing cornflower blue shorts and a white shirt, her fair hair tied with a blue ribbon.

She looked at Annys thoughtfully and wished she dared to ask her some questions. Could Annys possibly be her real mother? she wondered. Yet she looked so young, so very young. Mia felt more sure than ever that it was Phoebe who had eloped at seventeen, produced a baby, and been forced to give it away, remembering every year the baby's birthday and sending her a present.

Annys laughed. 'It is years since I baked or iced a cake.'

'Phoebe says we must do it secretly—that the men must not know whose cake they are buying. She says it'll be more fun that way.'

Annys laughed again. 'Trust Phoebe! Suppose I am landed with a terribly fat man and must dance with him?'

'You'll come to the dance?' Mia said eagerly.

Annys nodded. 'It is time I stopped the foolish business of fearing to meet people. Mia, I have tried to fight it, but it's only since I met you that I've learned to overcome it. You know my story, of course. Everyone on the island does. I have never been able to forgive myself—I feared to see other people because I thought they'd look at me with hatred because I killed the two people I loved most.' She lifted her hand. 'I know. It was not my fault. I have been told so many times. But the guilt remains.

'So I hid and then I could pretend it had not happened. But as Gideon said, one cannot hide for ever. I must face the truth and accept it. So—thanks to you, for I have seen no hatred or accusation in your eyes, Mia—I will come to the party.'

'I'm so glad,' Mia said eagerly.

She could not wait to tell Madame le Bret and Gideon, and when the carriage left her at the house she ran indoors, finding Gideon and his grandmother talking on the terrace.

Mia stood in the doorway, her cheeks flushed, her eyes bright. 'Madame le Bret,' she cried, 'Annys is coming to the dance and she's going to bake and ice a cake . . .'

Gideon stood up abruptly. 'She is?' he smiled. 'Good work, Mia.' For the moment, his cool hostility, that had lasted since the night he and Mia had spent in the cave, lifted as he looked at her. 'That's real progress,' he added. 'Isn't it, Grand'mère?'

Madame le Bret beamed. *'C'est si bon!* Our Contessa is coming back to life. It is indeed good, Mia my child.'

Mia had often iced cakes for the birthdays of children in the nursery school in which she had taught, so she tackled the job with experience, giving a great deal of thought to how she would ice it. She wanted the cake to be different—to make the children laugh. She decided to make the cake look like a Punch and Judy show, with the puppets made of icing and the children watching them of icing too. She went shopping to buy cochineal and other colouring, and the two days before the dance, was hard at work in a small pantry the butler had lent her.

Mia had always enjoyed icing and she hummed happily as she worked, watching the small figures come to life under her expert fingers. She stood back to examine the cake . . . the colours were gay and bright, and she heard a movement from the outer doorway.

She hurried and caught a glimpse of a tall man in a grey suit rounding the corner of the corridor. Gideon? Had he come to catch a glimpse of the cake? Why? It was not like him to cheat. But perhaps, she thought with a sudden misery, he wanted to find out which was her cake, so that he could be sure he would not accidentally buy it!

What had happened to spoil everything? He had been so wonderful on that dreadful day of the gale—and then had changed. The icy way he had said she had made it plain the sort of man she thought he was! Yet it had been a natural mistake she had made.

*   *   *

The children were thrilled with the cakes, crowding round to admire them. Phoebe was the auctioneer, standing on a small dais that Saturday afternoon, while the visitors to Le Bret Manor milled about.

The auction was gay—all the men bidding generously so that a tidy sum of money could be given to the orphans. The Contessa was there, keeping close to Gideon's side, looking exquisitely lovely, Mia thought, in a jade green silk suit and small matching hat of feathers. Annys looked frail, but she was laughing as she rested her hand on Gideon's arm and he smiled down at her. No wonder the Islanders believed he and Annys were in love, Mia thought with a sudden feeling of depression; just look at the way they smiled at one another! Perhaps now that Annys had admitted the world into her secret life, she would realise that Gideon loved her.

Suddenly the Punch and Judy cake was held high and Phoebe, her voice gay, asked for a bid.

There was a sudden silence and Gideon bid. Mia's heart seemed to skip. Gideon had seen her cake and was deliberately bidding for it, she thought. What did that mean?

Once started, the bidding rose briskly and Gideon's bidding had to rise higher and higher. Finally the cake went to Gideon, and Mia, watching them, saw him turn to Annys and say something.

Annys shook her head and pointed to the next cake, a delicate-looking garden of flowers made of icing. Beautifully designed, it was like a fairyland garden. Gideon looked startled and said something, and Annys nodded.

Mia turned away blindly. How could she have fooled herself? she thought miserably, as she escaped indoors and went to her room. Now she understood everything. Gideon had not seen her cake. If she had thought about it sensibly, she would have known that, she told herself. She had been standing over the cake, her back to the door. No one, not even a tall man like Gideon, could have seen the cake.

He had thought—for some unknown reason—that Annys had made the Punch and Judy cake. So he had bid for it and got it, and now he was landed with the wrong partner for the evening!

Who had won Annys's cake? she wondered. Questioning led her to the man, a plump bald-headed retired colonel, who was joking about it to his friends.

That night Mia wore a black chiffon frock. The pleated bodice hung in graceful folds over the waistline of the short flared skirt. She went to the dance in the carriage with Gideon and Madame le Bret, who had said she would like to watch for a few hours.

Once at the club house, as Gideon got Madame le Bret seated comfortably, Mia slipped away. The club grounds went down to the lagoon. The moon was high, the dark water had a silvery path. Mia sat on a rock and hugged her knees. With her out of the way, Gideon would be free. The colonel had high blood pressure and had openly admitted that he would only be able to dance once with the Contessa—which would mean that she, too, would be free.

A shadow fell across Mia and she looked up. Gideon was by her side. His eyes blazed, his mouth was a thin white line.

'Have you forgotten I bought you?' he said coldly.

Mia scrambled to her feet, smoothing the dress. 'I knew it was a mistake,' she said quickly. 'You thought it was Annys's cake, didn't you? I saw you asking her and she pointed to the one with flowers—the one you should have bought.'

'Why should I have bought it?' he asked.

Mia's cheeks were hot. 'Because you want to dance with Annys.'

'What makes you think that?'

'I—well, I—' she stammered, startled by the anger in his eyes.

'In any case, it is irrelevant,' Gideon said, his voice stiff. 'The point is that I bought your cake and everyone here knows it. Did you mean this as an open snub, a loud-voiced indication of the hatred you have for me?'

Mia's hand flew to her throat. 'I don't hate

you!'

His smile was grim. 'Don't bother to lie. It stands out a mile. You hate and despise me. Everything you do points to that. And now you want everyone to know, is that it?'

'Of course not—I thought it would help you, that you wanted to dance with Annys,' Mia stumbled. Whatever she said to Gideon was always wrong.

'Whether I want to dance with Annys or not is immaterial,' he said coldly. 'The point is—I bought your cake and I paid a good price for it, so I am determined to get my money's worth.' He held out his hand. 'Come, we're missing several dances already.'

Mia walked back slowly to the brilliantly decorated club house. Annys smiled as she danced by in the portly colonel's arms.

Gideon turned to Mia and she went into his arms. They danced, silently, without pleasure. In the intervals between music, they went and sat with Madame le Bret, behaving normally in front of her, neither of them wanting her to know how they felt.

Gideon was determined to get his pound of flesh, Mia thought miserably, as the evening passed. Never had she hated a dance so much. He danced well, as usual, but he held her with an impersonal casualness that was an insult in itself. His face was cold and grim, he gave no sign of enjoying the dance.

Later, Madame le Bret went home with

Annys, an Annys who had danced with every man save Gideon, for Gideon would not leave Mia's side.

Mia's head ached, her feet ached, but her heart ached most of all. How he must hate her, she thought miserably, punishing her for his mistake, making everyone talk about them and tease them. She could have wept for joy when the small band packed up and she and Gideon were driven home by a slightly drunk Pen, who insisted on singing the whole way back.

At the door of the house Gideon spoke.

'Thanks—for nothing, Mia,' he said, and turned away. 'I'll be gone in the morning before you're awake, so goodbye.'

Before Mia could speak, he had vanished, and she went miserably to her room.

She awoke to the sound of the roar of the plane as it took off and then circled above the island. Gideon had said nothing the day before about returning to England and she wondered at his decision and his early start. She found Madame le Bret a little sad but apparently having enjoyed the dance.

'My child, when you and Gideon dance, it is a beautiful sight. You are very *simpático*.'

Mia tried to smile. If you only knew the truth, she thought, if you knew how cruel Gideon had been, making me dance all the time, never asking if I was tired, never caring how miserable I was.

'Did Annys enjoy it? She left early,' she

asked.

Madame le Bret nodded. 'She told us before that she would not stay late. She said she enjoyed the dance very much.'

I'm glad,' said Mia. Glad someone had enjoyed the dance at any rate, she thought unhappily.

The children were leaving that day, so the hours sped by, filled with voices and laughter and tears. But at last the children were on the ship and Madame le Bret, Mia, Phoebe and Annys, stood on the quay waving their hankies in farewell.

'Come to tea with me, Madam le Bret,' Phoebe asked. 'Reg said he had not seen you for many months.'

Annys smiled. 'And Mia can come home with me, Madame le Bret. We have much to discuss.'

So it was arranged. Sitting in the white carriage drawn by the two black horses, Mia was asked by Annys how she had designed the Punch and Judy Show cake.

'It was delightful,' said Annys.

'Yours was much more beautiful,' Mia began, and hesitated. 'I'm terribly sorry about the mistake . . .'

Annys, coolly elegant in a cream sheath frock, looked puzzled. 'Mistake?' she queried.

Mia's cheeks were warm. 'Gideon bid for my cake by accident.'

Annys smiled. 'Did he? Whose cake did he

mean to bid for?'

'Yours,' Mia told her.

Annys laughed. 'How wrong you are, Mia. He knew which was my cake and that I didn't want to dance with him. Already on the island the matchmakers have been hard at work trying to marry me to Gideon. I said it would be more discreet if we did not dance the whole night together. I don't want my name linked with any man's on the island. He knew which was your cake, he told me. He saw it by chance in the house when you were icing it.'

Mia stared at her companion. 'You mean it wasn't a mistake? Did Gideon want to dance with me?'

'Of course. He says you are the best dancer he has ever met,' Annys laughed. 'My poor Mia, now I have made you blush!'

'It doesn't sound like Gideon.' Why had he wanted to dance with her? Mia wondered, and then she knew the reason. He had done it to protect Annys, to give the local people something fresh to talk about!

Annys laughed. 'You seem to have a strange idea of Gideon. He, too, can be gallant. Tell me, Mia,' Annys was grave, 'is it true what Gideon tells me—that you hate him?'

Again Mia's cheeks were burning. 'No, I don't,' she said vigorously, and then added more truthfully, 'But sometimes I think I do.'

Annys chuckled softly. 'He thinks you always do. What could there be to hate in a man like Gideon?'

Mia fidgeted unhappily. 'He is so arrogant at times, so sure he is always right.'

'He usually is,' Annys said quietly.

Mia turned to look at her. 'That only makes it worse.'

Annys began to laugh, and in the end Mia had to join in. It all sounded so childish. Annys touched Mia's hand gently.

'Men!' she said significantly. 'How difficult it is to understand them.'

The carriage stopped. The sun shone down at the pastel-coloured building, brightening the vivid colours of the flowers in the garden.

'This is a beautiful place, Annys.'

Annys nodded, her face sad. 'But a lonely one to enjoy by yourself,' she sighed. 'I think, perhaps, that Gideon is right and that I should go away for six months and see the world.'

'Gideon wants you to go away?' Mia asked, startled.

'Yes, he wants me to go to London and then, he says, he will make me remember that the only beauty in the world is not here. He says I should go to the theatre, the ballet, concerts, widen my horizons.'

'Perhaps he's right,' said Mia. She tried to imagine Gideon showing Annys the sights of London and the thought made her want to cry.

'As you said, Mia, it only makes it worse,' Annys said with a rueful smile. 'I was so happy here with my husband and my little child—I

227

came back to be near them, so that I could remember them, could see her running across the lawn, could picture him in the lagoon fishing. But perhaps Gideon is right and it is unhealthy to live in the past. But sometimes it's hard to leave it.' She paused, looked at Mia and smiled.

'Let's stop being mournful. Gideon brought me some new records I have not yet had time to hear. Shall we listen?'

'I'd love to,' said Mia.

*   *   *

How quiet life was without Gideon or the children, Mia thought as the days slipped by. Now it was no longer so stickily hot, a cool breeze would make the palm fronds dance and toss their heads gaily, the lagoon water would ripple with a thousand tiny waves, the birds seemed to sing much louder, and Mia was no nearer solving her problem than she had been on the day of her arrival on the island.

She still felt that her real mother must be Phoebe—yet she still could not bring herself to precipitate a crisis and break her promise to her father by telling Phoebe the truth.

Having decided to tell no one that it was her birthday, Mia still felt desolate when she awoke and there were no cards or presents. At home, her father had always made her birthday a very special day, taking her out to

228

dinner and a show, buying her something she really needed, and obviously enjoying their day together as much as she did.

Now, as the morning dragged by, although Mia knew it was her own fault for not telling anyone—indeed, she had been silent in case the news might have triggered off the truth, and perhaps the time was not yet ripe for that—she felt miserable, and when Annys phoned to ask her for lunch, Mia—knowing some special friends of Madame le Bret were lunching with her—gratefully accepted.

Sitting in the sunlit courtyard before lunch, Annys talked of her little girl, her face sad. After lunch—delicious as usual—Annys and Mia lay on long comfortable couches in the shade and listened to Annys's favourite records.

Unexpectedly Annys said: 'Mia, you never wear your ring these days. Aren't you going to marry Ian?'

It was the first personal question Annys had ever asked Mia. 'No. I—I haven't told Gideon but I broke off the engagement some time ago.'

Annys looked surprised. 'Why?'

Mia told her the whole story. 'I was in love with Ian—I'd always known him and we were so happy together, but then when he left the university and went to work for his father, he changed.'

She tried to make Annys see the new Ian,

trying to do the right thing, following his parents' example.

'His parents were,' Mia tried to laugh—'were grooming me to be the right kind of wife. Annys, I'd be no good. I went to one dance—they gave it to announce our engagement, and everything was wrong. I was expected to be nice to boring people, especially nice to—'

'Gideon?' Annys said with a smile. 'He told me how miserable you looked. Was that how you met?'

Mia nodded. 'Yes, he told me not to marry Ian, that he was a "mother's boy".'

'And that made you mad?' Annys said with a laugh.

Mia nodded. 'I hated Gideon for it. It was only later that I realised how right he was, but I had never seen it.'

'Why haven't you told Gideon the engagement is off?' Annys asked casually.

Mia hesitated. 'Well, it's really . . .' Then she drew a deep breath. 'I might as well be honest. I hate to have to admit that he was right,' she said miserably.

Annys looked at her. 'Are you afraid he'll crow about it?'

Mia nodded.

Annys tried to smile. 'Oh, Mia, one day you'll grow up!'

Mia lifted her head. 'I'm twenty, today.'

'It's your birthday?' Annys sat up, hugging her knees, resting her pointed chin on them.

She was wearing a gaily-coloured sarong. 'That's funny,' she began, and then stopped. 'How old were you when you met—what's his name?—oh yes, Ian?'

'I must have been about six years old,' Mia told her, 'but I didn't fall in love with him until I was seventeen.'

Annys lay down, linking her arms behind her head. 'Seventeen—a wonderful age,' she said dreamily. 'I remember when I was seventeen, Mia. I was at the finishing school in Lucerne. In winter we used to practise winter sports. I met a medical student. He was eighteen, in his first year. We fell in love . . .'

Mia turned to watch Annys's face. Annys had closed her eyes, was speaking softly, as if what she was saying, was too precious to talk about loudly or clumsily.

'We eloped to Gretna Green,' Annys went on, and Mia sat up abruptly, holding her breath as she watched the beautiful face with its lovely features and delicate skin. 'We knew our parents would never let us marry. He had five brothers and they had little money. My parents were wealthy and had ambitious plans for me, but we loved one another . . .' Her voice seemed to caress the words.

'I thought that once it was a *fait accompli* my parents would accept it and let us lead our own lives. How wrong I was,' she said bitterly. 'They sent the police after us. Peter was jailed. The marriage was annulled and I was whisked off to Spain.'

'Spain?' Mia whispered. She did not dare move. She had to know the whole truth.

'Yes, I had a baby. A little girl.' Annys's voice was unsteady. 'It's funny, she would have been twenty years old today . . .'

And in England, there is a parcel waiting for that little girl, Mia thought, suddenly near tears. The birthday parcel you send every year for the daughter you have never stopped loving, the daughter who is here by your side . . .

'I'll never forget her,' Annys went on softly. 'It broke my heart to part with her, but they were right. I was not eighteen, what sort of mother would I have made? My child went to a couple who were mature and well-to-do. She would never want for love or for food. But that's another guilt I feel, Mia. I shall never know if I did the right or wrong thing. Maybe she needs me—my parents always told me I must never get in touch with her, that it would be cruel to her and unfair to the people who love her.'

'And—and the medical student?' asked Mia. Her father! It was strange to think that a boy of eighteen had been her father.

'He died. We never met again and he died in a car accident about a year later. I don't think he even knew I had had a child,' said Annys. 'I was terribly unhappy for a long time and then I met Antonio Severini. He was

232

gentle and kind and my parents wanted me to marry him. So I did. But I did not love him. That came later, gradually. He was a wonderful man . . .'

Mia was trying to find the right words. What should she do or say? Should she cry out 'Mother!' dramatically—or should she break the news gently? Say that she had been adopted, that she had been born in Spain . . .

She looked at Annys's beautiful sad face and felt a flood of proud love sweep through her. My mother. This beautiful woman is my mother, she thought. My very own real mother . . .

'. . . I,' she began, but a door slammed and Annys sat up. Mia's cheeks had gone white, for Gideon came striding out of the house.

'Gideon!' Annys was on her feet in a second, almost running to meet him. 'I didn't expect you for another week.'

He took both her hands in his and smiled down at her. 'I brought the records you want,' he said. 'I had a job getting them, but I couldn't wait to see your face.'

Annys was radiant with happiness. 'You are a darling, Gideon. I can never thank you enough. I've been longing to get them.'

Mia sat still, watching them. She had never felt so embarrassed or in the way. Not that they were aware of her. From the way they stood close together, Annys's hands in Gideon's, gazing into one another's eyes, no

233

one else in the world existed.

Mia wondered what to do. Creep away? Surely that would be worse. Just sit there, feeling redundant and unwanted?

The joyous warmth that had filled her when she knew that Annys was her mother for whom she had been searching had vanished.

How could she, Mia asked herself, tell Gideon that his beloved and beautiful Annys had a daughter of twenty? How could she reveal herself to Annys, embarrass her by making her real age apparent, for Annys looked little more than thirty, but must be, in reality, thirty-seven.

Gideon was a strange man. He might find it impossible to forgive Annys for her deception, for not telling him bout the child she had had when she was seventeen. He might find it hard to accept the role of stepfather to a girl of twenty, and that might ruin their whole relationship, Mia thought worriedly. She loved Gideon with all her heart and even though it hurt to know he loved another woman, yet in all the world he could not have chosen anyone nicer than Annys. And when you love someone, Mia told herself, you can only want their happiness.

It was the same where Annys was concerned. Mia loved her with the aching longing she had known ever since she discovered she was an adopted child and that her mother had loved her enough to send her an anonymous present every year. But loving Annys meant surely that Mia wanted Annys's happiness—and that was obviously with Gideon.

Annys turned, dropping Gideon's hands. 'How rude we are, Mia,' she said gaily. 'Isn't it lovely to have Gideon back?'

'Yes . . .' Mia managed to say. She looked at the tall, broad-shouldered man in the cream linen suit, the immaculate matching shirt and deep blue silk tie. She loved him so much that her whole body seemed to ache with desolation—for he was not for her. He loved her mother, and the best way she could help them both, she knew with a sudden stricken honesty, was to leave the island as soon as she could do so, without making it seem obvious. 'Madame le Bret doesn't expect you. I didn't hear the plane . . .'

'It didn't come,' Gideon explained. 'I met a friend in Mombasa who was coming in his yacht, so I joined him. Made a nice change.'

Annys was clapping her hands and a maid came running, to be given orders and vanish. 'You must have a drink before you go, Gideon.'

Mia sat quietly as they drank and talked. She was careful to act normally, to join in the conversation when necessary, to laugh at the right moments, but the tears were beginning to grow inside her and she longed for the quiet sanctuary of her room where she could weep for the mother she had found and immediately lost.

In the carriage going home, she decided she was tired of lying to Gideon. Let him be triumphant and crow if he wanted to, she thought, only hoping it would not make her break down and cry.

'I've broken off my engagement with Ian,' she said abruptly.

Gideon turned, his face stiff. 'I know. Ian came to see me. You broke it off some time ago, Mia. Why did you lie to me?'

She smoothed out the skirt of her buttercup yellow cotton frock and did not look at him for a moment. Then she lifted her head and stared at him. 'Because you were right and I hated to admit it,' she said honestly.

He looked startled. 'But—but . . .'

'I know,' Mia said wearily. 'It's time I grew up and had some sense. It was childish of me and I admit it. Maybe I'll soon get some sense, though, for I'm twenty today.'

Gideon smiled. 'Really? Happy birthday, then.'

'Thank you,' she said, and turned quickly before he could see the tears in her eyes. It was the unhappiest birthday of her life.

CHAPTER ELEVEN

After a restless, unhappy night, Mia awoke to hear the wind suddenly rising in strength, tearing at the palm leaves. She dressed quickly and went outside, running down to the lagoon. Its usual serene beauty had vanished, now the smooth water was a chaos of white-flecked waves. The wind whipped at the sand, stinging her cheeks painfully.

Mia felt like the water—frustrated, fighting for escape. Somehow—if only she could find a way—she must leave the island as soon as possible, she decided. It would be too difficult to keep the secret. An odd word, a revealing slip in the conversation, and she could betray everything.

What could she do? she wondered. If she hadn't told Gideon the truth about Ian, she could have said she wanted to go back to him. But then Gideon had already known the truth about the broken engagement and he would have told her so. What plan could she make?

The next time she was in the township, she managed to slip away from Pen and into the small tourist bureau. She asked about cruising liners that might call in the near future, but there were none for three months. There was no means of going by ship, she was told, unless she got a lift on one of the big yachts that called in fairly frequently. There was one in now called *Apollo*. Mia knew it must be the yacht Gideon had come on, but she wanted to ask no favours of him or of his friends.

She went to see Phoebe and explained her desire not to ask Gideon for help. 'I still haven't paid my fare to Mombasa,' she explained unhappily. 'Whenever I talk to Gideon about it, he tells me to tell his secretary to send out an account. I did, but she hasn't.'

'Why does it worry you, Mia?' Phoebe asked. 'Being indebted to Gideon, I mean.'

It was strange, Mia thought, but she liked Phoebe just as much, even though now she knew that she was not her mother. Phoebe had always been so easy to talk to, but now Mia hesitated. 'I—I don't know . . .'

Phoebe smiled sympathetically. 'Stronger women than you have fallen for him, Mia. Is that the trouble? You want to run away before you get too involved?'

Mia looked at her miserably. 'Is it so obvious?'

Phoebe laughed. 'I don't think so. Gideon wouldn't notice it in any case, for he's one of the least conceited men I know.'

'I—' Mia hesitated. Should she tell Phoebe, she wondered, of the little scene between Gideon and Annys, when they had held hands, gazed into one another's eyes and had so obviously forgotten the world?

238

That moment had told Mia the truth—that Gideon loved Annys and Annys loved Gideon.

'I'm glad,' she said. 'I'd hate him to know.'

'I wish you hadn't to,' said Phoebe. 'Madame le Bret will miss you, but I know how you feel. It's better to run away before it's too late and you break your heart.'

Mia fidgeted with the green cord tied round the waist of her white frock, keeping her eyes hidden from Phoebe.

'That's how I feel, Phoebe,' she said, but it was not the whole truth.

It was already too late and her heart had been broken. Now she must pick up the pieces, find the courage to escape and go to a new world, meeting new people, building up a new life.

'I think you'll have to tell Gideon and ask for a lift,' Phoebe said thoughtfully, 'there's no other way for some time.'

'I know,' Mia admitted unhappily.

*   *   *

That evening, Gideon suggested a walk by the moon-lit lagoon. The wind had dropped and everything was still. Mia would have refused, but Madame le Bret smiled approvingly and wished them goodnight.

It was very quiet outside except for the ever-constant distant roar of the waves breaking on the reef in helpless fury, as they had beaten against it for centuries. The huge palm trees did not move but were silhouetted against a star-bright, moonlit sky.

Mia looked round. How could she bear to leave this paradise, she asked herself, and all her new friends whom she had grown to love; Madame le Bret, Phoebe, Pen. And now her real mother, Annys.

'It's so beautiful,' she said gently as they stood on a rock hanging out over the gentle lagoon and watched the reflections of the palm trees in the still water.

'And yet you want to leave,' said Gideon.

Startled, she turned too quickly and nearly fell off the flat rock. Only Gideon's quick hand that caught her arm and steadied her saved her from the fall. She would not have drowned, she knew that, but she certainly would have looked silly lying in six inches of water!

'You know . . . ?' she said.

Gideon's face looked hard and unfriendly. 'Pen is an inquisitive old boy. He saw you go into the tourist bureau and is upset. He says Grand'mère will break her heart when you go.'

Mia bit her lip. 'I can't stay here for ever.'

Gideon took out his cigarette case, offered her a cigarette, lit it for her, and then lit one for himself. 'Getting bored?' he asked curtly.

Mia's cheeks were hot. 'Of course not,' she said hastily. 'I love it here, but . . .'

He looked at her. 'But . . . ?'

She thought wildly. If only he would stop

240

looking at her like that! His steel-grey eyes seemed able to look right into her mind. If he knew the truth, she thought. If he knew she was only going because she loved him so much—and because of Annys, her real mother. If he only knew how hard this was for her. How difficult it was to be unselfish and want them to find happiness together.

'Where d'you think of going?' Gideon asked. 'You won't want to go back to Hawbridge, and you'll hate London.'

'I—I might go somewhere new,' Mia said wildly.

Gideon frowned. 'Were you perhaps thinking of the island called Mahé?' he asked, his voice sarcastic. 'Why not tell the truth for once, Mia. Admit you want to see Toby Caldecoot again, don't you?'

Mia caught her breath. 'Toby? Oh, Toby! I . . .' She grasped at it like a drowning man clutching at a passing branch. 'Yes, I do,' she said quickly, 'he's good fun, and . . .'

'I'm not?' Gideon spoke so quietly that for a moment Mia wondered if she had heard him properly. She stared up at him. His eyes were narrowed, his mouth a thin line.

'You—you're different,' she stammered.

'In what way?' he enquired politely. 'I realise that I am older than Toby Caldecoot, also that I am not the type of man to flirt with an engaged girl, but I am definitely a better dancer and a much more eligible proposition.'

241

Mia's cheeks blazed with anger. 'You're always suggesting I'm looking for a husband with money!'

'Aren't you? Most girls are,' he said with an odd smile.

Mia bit her lower lip. 'When—if—' she swallowed and began again. 'If I love a man, I don't care if he hasn't got a penny,' she said angrily. 'Money means everything to you—to me, it means nothing.'

'Only because you've never starved,' Gideon said coolly.

She began to speak, then stopped. Perhaps he was right. She had never been hungry, so how could she judge? As usual, she thought wearily, he was right.

'I don't know why or how this started,' she said. 'I'm merely saying that I think it's time I moved on. Much as I love your grandmother, Gideon, I'll have to go one day. The longer I stay, the harder it'll be to go.'

He gave her an odd look. 'You could be right. Is there any urgency? I mean d'you want to go tomorrow, next week or next month? It's my grandmother's birthday in two weeks' time, we're already planning a big party. I'd be grateful if you'd stay for that.'

'Of course I will,' she said.

Carefully she stepped off the rocks on to the sand, but Gideon's hand was already under her elbow. The touch of his warm hand on her bare skin made her tremble. She had to stiffen

242

herself, blink her eyes fast as they walked up towards the house.

'I'm sorry you feel you must go,' Gideon said quietly, his voice faintly sad.

'So am I,' said Mia. Her voice thickened and, terrified lest she burst into tears, she ran the rest of the way to the house, and Gideon made no attempt to follow her.

*   *   *

Mia, Gideon and Annys were sitting on the lawn outside the house when they heard the distant roar of the aeroplane. They had met to discuss Madame le Bret's birthday party.

Annys wanted them to give the old lady a surprise. 'I don't know what she likes, but let's make it a special party,' Annys said eagerly.

Mia, sitting quietly, joining in now and then, looked at her mother. Had there ever been a nicer or more beautiful woman? Mia wondered. Now, in a simple straight cream frock, Annys looked elegant enough to be presented at Court, she thought, feeling frumpish and dowdy in her blue sheath frock. Annys had changed so much, Mia was thinking. The lost look had gone from her eyes which now sparkled as she laughed, her pale cheeks were flushed, she looked alive and happy.

Gideon looked up at the sky with a frown. 'It sounds like my plane, but I'm not expecting anyone,' he said, and stood up. 'I'd better send Pen up. I won't be a moment,' he added, and left them.

'Is Gideon staying for his grandmother's birthday?' Mia asked.

Annys smiled at her. 'Yes.' Her face clouded. 'I'm sorry you have to go, Mia, we'll miss you. Is—' she hesitated—'is this Toby a nice man?'

'Toby?' Mia echoed, and flushed. 'Oh, Toby! Yes, very nice, good fun. Amusing.'

'But what will you do in Victoria? It's a small town and the whole island of Mahé isn't very big. Won't you—' Annys hesitated. 'It's not my business . . .'

It is your business, Mia cried out silently. If only she could tell Annys the truth!

Gideon came back, looking puzzled. He wore white shorts and a shirt and looked, as usual, clean and cool. 'That's funny,' he said, 'it is my plane, so some crisis must have occurred.'

'They could phone,' Annys said.

Gideon shrugged. 'It's never very satisfactory. I prefer them to come out and talk to me. Anyhow, Pen's gone up to meet him, so we can relax. Now what were we saying . . . ?'

They were still discussing the party when they heard the gentle clop-clop of Nero's hooves and the tinkling bell that hung from his comical little straw hat. From where they sat, they could hear voices and then the staccato tap of high heels, and all turned to look at the terrace.

Gwyneth Vaughan stood there, blinking in the bright sunshine. Gideon's personal assistant looked, Mia thought, instantly, as beautifully glamorous as ever. Today she wore a bluebell mauve shantung suit with a huge cream handbag and high-heeled shoes.

'Gideon . . .?' she said. 'I can't see you properly. I left my dark glasses behind. It was raining in London and like an idiot, I forgot the sun always shines out here.' She came down towards them. Under one arm she had an umbrella which she dropped on the ground and looked at Mia. 'You are still here?' she said. 'Good, I . . .'

'Why have you come, Miss Vaughan?' Gideon asked, his voice so cold that Mia shivered.

Gwyneth Vaughan looked startled, for a moment ill at ease, but then she recovered. 'It's the Johnson merger, Gideon. Something new came up, and when we heard you weren't coming back for several weeks, we decided one of us should come out and talk it over with you,' she said briskly.

'The Johnson merger has been settled long ago,' Gideon said. 'I cabled to tell you so. It's off.'

'Off?' Gwyneth frowned. 'But we've had no cable, and they contacted us . . .'

'Miss Vaughan must be weary, Gideon,' Annys said quietly. 'Won't you ask her to sit down and order some tea? You can discuss business later.'

At the sound of the voice, Gwyneth swung round and stared at the Contessa as if only seeing her there for the first time. A strange expression flitted over Gwyneth's face that puzzled Mia. It looked cunning yet triumphant, startled yet pleased.

'You must be the beautiful but mysterious Contessa,' Gwyneth said, and sat down while Gideon shouted towards the house an order.

Annys smiled serenely. 'And you must be the capable Girl Friday Gideon is always talking about.'

Gideon had fetched an extra chair, now he straddled it, facing the three of them, his eyes narrowed as he watched Gwyneth open her huge bag and bring out a small parcel.

'Mia,' said Gwyneth, 'you did live at Hawbridge vicarage, didn't you? And you are Miss Barton?'

Mia caught her breath, shocked into stillness, staring at the parcel in Gwyneth's hand. Mia managed to nod and Gwyneth went on: 'This was delivered there and the new vicar gave it to Ian, believing you were still engaged to him. Ian brought it to the office, so I thought as I was coming out . . .'

Mia jumped as Annys leaned forward and touched her hand. Annys's eyes were wide with wonder. 'Mia, I never heard your surname before. Are you Miss Barton?'

Mia's mouth was dry with fear as she nodded. How could she stop this? She put out her hand took the parcel.

'Thanks,' she said.

Gwyneth laughed gaily. 'Don't thank me, I didn't send it. Thank the Contessa. I recognised her very original handwriting at once and the green ink, as well as the postmark,' she finished triumphantly.

Mia stared at her for a moment. Never, Mia thought, had she seen such an evil smile before. Gwyneth obviously knew nothing, but she had seen it as a chance to damage Annys in Gideon's eyes, to make Annys appear deceitful, because surely he would wonder why Annys and Mia had pretended not to know one another when Annys must have already posted the parcel to her?

Annys's hand tightened round Mia's, so Mia turned to look at the beautiful face near hers. Annys's eyes were full of tears. 'Then Mia . . . Mia darling, you are my child,' she said softly.

Mia's smile was shaky. 'Yes—Mother,' she said very gently, loving the feel of the word on her lips.

'Oh, darling . . . darling!' Annys stood up and held Mia close, bending to kiss her, straightening to look at Gideon. 'Gideon, isn't it wonderful?' she said eagerly. 'This is my baby—the baby I told you about . . .'

'Mia—your *child*?' Gwyneth interrupted, her face startled.

Annys turned to her immediately. 'Yes. I was seventeen when I eloped, but my parents broke up the marriage and made me let the baby be adopted. I hated it!'

'Yes,' said Mia, holding Annys's hand tightly, 'my father . . .'

'You knew you were adopted, Mia?' Gideon interrupted.

Mia turned to him. 'Not until the day he was knocked down by a car. He was worried, as he'd always wanted to tell me, but his wife didn't want me to know. She was afraid . . . afraid I'd love them less, perhaps, but I couldn't. They were wonderful to me. But he—he felt I should know because he—he seemed to know he was going to—to die and he said my real mother still loved me . . .'

'She gave you away,' Gwyneth said quickly.

Mia looked at her. 'She was seventeen and they made her believe it was the right thing to do.' She turned to Annys. 'D'you know why they called me Mia?' she asked. 'It was at the Spanish convent. They had called to fetch me and they heard you sobbing bitterly and saying, "She's mine—mine—mine," so they called me Mia.' She paused for breath. She was speaking fast, determined to say it all before Gwyneth could interrupt with some unkind remark.

'He said he knew you loved me, Annys,' Mia went on, 'because every birthday you sent me a

248

present. I never knew who it was from—he told me it was from my godmother. They were lovely presents,' she went on rapidly, 'the most beautiful things . . .'

As she spoke, her hands trembled as she tore open the parcel and brought out a small, exquisitely designed tortoiseshell fan. She stood up and kissed Annys.

'Thank you,' she said, her voice suddenly breaking. 'Thank you so very much . . .'

Annys's arms were tightly round her. 'My baby . . .' she said, trying to laugh, the laughter mixed with tears. 'All this time I never knew—'

Gideon frowned. 'But how did you know Annys was your mother, Mia? Is that why you came out here?'

Mia nodded. 'I had to come. When I—I learned the truth, I felt I had to find my mother. My father had said he kept the stamps—that my mother must have moved round the world, but that for the last three years the postmark had been the same. He wanted me to wait for my next birthday in case she had moved again. I guess I would have waited if he—if he hadn't died. But I had to find her.'

'Why didn't you tell me?' demanded Gideon.

'Because he made me promise not to. He said it might be embarrassing.'

'I'll say!' Gwyneth broke in quickly. 'To look as young as the Contessa does and suddenly be confronted with a grown-up daughter could be most embarrassing,' she said in a nasty voice.

Annys laughed. 'How right you are! The saving grace being that I longed to find my daughter. To find my daughter . . . I, too, Mia, had made a promise. I went to the priest in the Spanish village and asked for your new name. He gave it to me on condition I gave my word of honour I would never let you know I was your mother. He said it would be cruel to you and unfair to your adoptive parents. So I had to be content with the birthday presents. I'm glad you liked them.'

'I loved them,' Mia said warmly.

'When did you know Annys was your mother?' Gideon asked, his voice quiet.

Mia hesitated. Thinking fast, she recognised the pit-falls here, for she mustn't say the wrong thing. 'On my birthday. Annys told me about her baby and how sad she was, and when she said the baby was born in Spain exactly twenty years before, I couldn't be wrong.'

'But, darling, why didn't you tell me then?' Annys said. 'It would have made me so happy.'

'But Mia wasn't to know that, was she, Contessa?' said Gwyneth, her voice amused. 'You appear to be about thirty, very beautiful and also eligible as a wealthy woman. Perhaps Mia was afraid of spoiling your marriage prospects if she forced you to admit openly that she was your child.'

'Miss Vaughan,' Gideon's voice was icily

cold, 'you forget yourself. You owe the Contessa an apology.'

Annys shook her head. 'Please, Gideon, take no notice. She did not mean to be insulting, so don't spoil this beautiful day for me. Mia, let's go and tell Madame le Bret the wonderful news shall we?'

Hand in hand, Mia and her real mother walked up the terrace steps, into the cool darkness of the house. In the hall, Annys turned to kiss Mia.

'You can't think how happy I am, Mia.'

'Me, too,' smiled Mia, blinking fast. 'Oh, Annys, please never feel guilty about me. You did the best thing. I had such a happy childhood, such darling parents, and now that I've lost them, I've got you.' She paused. 'I'm so happy, so very happy!'

It was the truth. Gideon knew everything and he still loved Annys. So having Annys as her mother, Mia knew, would make no difference. Annys and Gideon could marry and be happy.

Then—quite suddenly—Mia knew something. Something so difficult to face, so hard to accept, and yet she must accept—the simple, unpalatable truth that Gideon would be her stepfather.

CHAPTER TWELVE

'Is it true?' Madame le Bret cried, her face flushed, her eyes shining. 'Mia is your child, Annys? How can this be?'

'It is true,' Annys said happily.

Perhaps for the third or even for the fourth time both Mia and Annys had to start at the beginning and tell the old lady their stories again.

Madame le Bret touched her wet eyes with her lace-edged hankie. 'My poor Annys, you were so young and wept so much for your child . . .'

'I could never forget her—I was never sure if I'd done the right thing,' said Annys.

'And every year she sent me a beautiful present,' Mia put in.

When Gideon joined them, his face was grim, but he relaxed with his grandmother, that being a very special day.

'We must celebrate,' the old lady said gaily. 'I will order a special dinner.'

Gideon turned to Annys. 'Could we dine at your place? It would simplify matters.'

Annys smiled. 'Of course. Anything you say, Gideon. And Miss Vaughan?'

A cloud seemed to pass over his face. 'Dinner will be served in her room. She's flying back first thing tomorrow,' he said curtly.

Mia wondered what he had said to Gwyneth. He had been furious with her when she insulted Annys. And Gwyneth had obviously lied about the cable and the merger. Why had she come? Why had she risked Gideon's anger? The parcel could have been forwarded by post—why had it to be delivered in person?

Mia felt the only solution could be Gwyneth's obvious desire to hurt and embarrass Annys. Maybe Ian had talked—had said Mia was looking for her mother on the island. Could Gwyneth, recognising the green ink and Annys's flowing writing, have taken a chance and come out to see what trouble she could make? Even if Gwyneth had not guessed the truth—that Annys was Mia's mother—she might have thought Gideon would be angry with Annys if he learned she already knew Mia well enough to send her a present and yet neither Annys or Mia had mentioned it.

Mia shivered. It was her fault, she knew. She had told Gwyneth that the islanders thought Gideon was in love with Annys, and so Gwyneth had taken measures to hurt Annys.

Mia shivered again. It showed how easily a word said carelessly or—as in her case, cattily—could hurt people. How disastrous it might have been had Gideon not known the truth—that Annys had given birth to a child when she was seventeen years of age.

Lunch was gay. Afterwards Madame le Bret

insisted that Mia stay with Annys. 'The position is now reversed,' she said gaily. 'Every day you can visit me, Mia.'

A wave of excitement seemed to go through the lovely villa as the staff learned that Miss Mia was really the Contessa's daughter whom she had not seen since she was a baby. A luxurious bedroom was prepared. That night Annys and Mia sat up talking until the small hours; they had so much to learn about one another, so much to say.

Mia soon adjusted herself to her new life, being shuttled to and fro between Le Bret Manor and the Italian villa. Always Gideon and Madame le Bret dined with them. News had spread round the island and congratulations and good wishes poured in.

Phoebe hugged Mia and Mia confessed: 'I used to think you were my mother, Phoebe.'

Phoebe sighed and said sadly: 'I wish I could have been, Mia, but I have never had a child.'

Madame le Bret's birthday approached and plans for the party grew.

'We must make it a day she will never forget,' Annys said affectionately.

Their plans were kept secret, but Annys and Gideon whispered a lot, laughing in a conspiratorial way, smiling across the room with the specially significant smile Mia was beginning to recognise—and to dread, for it made her heart ache so badly.

How, Mia constantly asked herself, was she

going to bear it—living with Gideon and Annys when they were married? How could she endure watching them together? Yet how, she wondered, could she refuse to live with them? What excuse could she give?

Mia was commissioned to take Madame le Bret shopping the afternoon before the party so that Gideon and Annys could prepare everything. It was a pleasant day as Mia and Madame le Bret were driven along the coast road to the township. A breeze off the ocean cooled the hot air and the trees were bright with flowers.

Staring at the fascinating harbour with the mountain towering above it, Mia sighed. How was she going to bear it when they got married?

'You are so quiet, my child,' Madame le Bret observed. 'What were you thinking about?'

Without realising it, Mia continued her thoughts out loud. 'I was wondering when the wedding will be.'

'Whose wedding, dear child?' Madame le Bret asked, her voice soft.

'Their wedding, of course . . .' Mia suddenly realised that she had been thinking aloud. Hand flying to her mouth, she stared at Madame le Bret. 'Nobody knows about it yet.'

The old lady, elegant in her straw hat and royal blue frock, looked mystified. 'Then how do you?'

'I can see it—when they look at one another. The way he says her name, the way she smiles . . .'

'Mia, are you sick, my child? I think your mind is wandering. Who is he and who is she?' Madame le Bret asked.

Mia's eyes widened.

'Gideon and—and Annys's wedding, I mean,' she explained.

The old lady's face was worried. 'Are you sure, child? Has Annys spoken to you about it—or Gideon?'

The carriage jolted them as it bumped over a bad piece of road, and Mia shook her head. 'No—but I can see it.'

Madame le Bret relaxed. 'My child, you see what you think you see. For a moment, you had me worried, but I am certain that Gideon and Annys do not plan to marry. She has an Italian suitor. He writes twice a week, but she would not marry him. She said she was too sick—too afraid of the world. Perhaps now it will be different.'

'But you said once that you were afraid Gideon would marry Annys,' Mia said, and then looked self-consciously at Pen's back, his pointed cat's ears alert.

Madame le Bret nodded understandingly, leant forward, touching Pen's back gently with the ferrule of her blue silk sunshade, and ordered him to drive them to the seats under the trees near the bandstand by the quay where they could have tea.

'We can sit there and talk while Pen does our shopping,' the old lady said.

Later, sitting in the shade, sipping tea, Madame le Bret reopened the conversation: 'My child, I was only afraid that Gideon, out of the kindness of his heart, might fall in love with Annys. She was frail, pathetic and that is Gideon's weak point—his compassion for others. I thought Annys might marry him if she was desperately unhappy, but I hoped not, for I believed that her feeling of guilt would make her punish Gideon. But now she is a new woman—young, gay, happy. You have cured her of the feeling of guilt, my child. Annys told me only yesterday that she has written to ask Giovanni here for a visit. She wants you to meet him, for he would, of course, be your stepfather.'

Mia turned to look at the old lady. 'But I am so sure that Gideon loves her.'

Madame le Bret gave a funny little smile. 'Remember, Mia, I said once that you had made Gideon your whipping boy?' Mia nodded. 'I also said that there were many things about Gideon that you did not understand?'

Mia nodded again, puzzled by the old lady's words. 'You love him, don't you?' Madame le Bret demanded.

Mia caught her breath at the bluntness of the question. 'Yes,' she said quietly. 'That's why.'

'That's why you were going away? Why didn't you tell Annys you were her daughter—because you were afraid it might anger Gideon and you thought he loved her?' Madame le Bret asked gently.

Mia nodded. 'I—I want them to be happy.'

'They will be—but not your way, Mia. Their way. Dear child—' Madame le Bret's voice changed as she covered Mia's hot hand with hers—'are you so blind? Don't you know that from the first Gideon has loved you?'

'Loved me?' Mia's hand went to her throat, her face was dismayed. 'I'm sure he doesn't. He's always criticising me, treats me as a child . . .'

Madame le Bret was smiling. 'And you find him arrogant, rude, impossible and hateful—at times. Am I right?'

Mia nodded. 'He is so moody. He can be nice and so hateful. So kind and so cruel.'

'So can you, my child,' said Madame le Bret. 'You have hurt him deeply, perhaps without realising the depth of the pain, and so he hates you. Just as you hate him when you think he is cruel to you.'

'But . . .'

The old lady lifted her hand. '*Un moment*, please, Mia. Love and hate walk hand in hand. He who loves the most can also hate the most. It is not the "hate" you read about in the dictionary which says "to dislike intensely", but the quick hatred which is the swing of the pendulum from love. You are hurt by the one you love—so you hate him. In turn you hurt him, so he hates you. But deep in your hearts there is only love. The hatred is a form of self-defence, an armour.'

'But—but—Madame le Bret,' Mia could hardly speak, 'd'you honestly think Gideon loves me?' Her voice had an awed, rapt sound as if it was too wonderful to be true.

'I am sure of it. So is Annys. We were laughing yesterday when she said that soon she would indeed be old with a son-in-law only four years younger than herself. We were saying that Gideon's frequent visits should have told us—if nothing else. Never before has he come so often in so short a time.'

'She thinks Gideon loves me?' Mia repeated slowly. 'I can't believe it. He's never shown any sign of even liking me.'

'Hasn't he?' Madame le Bret said gently. 'Think. Try to remember how hurt and angry he was when you vanished at the dance and he had bought your cake. Didn't he ask you once why you hated him? He has told me several times that he finds you hard to understand.'

'As I do him,' Mia said very slowly. She leaned over the table and clutched the thin frail hand. 'You're not just saying this? It's really true?' she said eagerly.

'I knew when he brought you to my house. Gideon would not have brought any girl

259

home. He would have found you some accommodation. When I saw you, I could have wept with joy. You are just the sort of girl for Gideon. You will be a wonderful granddaughter . . .' Suddenly the happiness went out of the elderly face. 'But you are proud, and Gideon is proud, too. He believes you love this boy called Toby.'

'I only said I wanted to see Toby to have an excuse to leave him alone with Annys,' Mia confessed.

'Then you must tell Gideon so. You must be the one to make the first move, Mia. Gideon believed you to be engaged—then to be in love with this Toby. So long as he believes that, he cannot tell you of his love.'

Mia's cheeks were hot. 'But how could I tell him?'

Madame le Bret smiled. 'We will make a plan, my child. Let us think. First we must find Gideon's Achilles heel. Every man and woman has one. Ah, I think I mentioned it earlier— Gideon's weakness is compassion. If someone is in trouble or difficulty, he is—not weak, but prepared to listen to them. You must be in trouble, Mia . . .'

Mia began to laugh and stopped because the sound got perilously hysterical. 'But how can I be in trouble?'

How could she tell Gideon she loved him? she asked herself. Face those thoughtful, shrewd grey eyes and say, 'I love you, Gideon.'

Waiting for his amusement, his contempt, his scathing word. Suppose his grandmother was wrong, and he did not love her?

'Mia, I know what we must do.' Madame le Bret lowered her voice, her eyes twinkling. 'Tonight after dinner you must take a stroll down to the lagoon. I will employ Gideon with chess. Then when you have had time I will be alarmed and will send him in search of you. Do not let it be too easy to find you, Mia. Cling to him when he does. Weep a little. Then tell him softly that you lied about Toby, that it was because you thought he loved Annys. The rest will follow.'

Mia gazed at the old lady in dismay. 'I couldn't do that. It would be dishonest.'

Madame le Bret shook her head. 'Is it dishonest to love a man and want his happiness? Is it a crime to help a man overcome his pride so that he may gain his heart's desire? Think about it, my child, and if you truly love Gideon, you will find the strength and skill required. Love will always find a way. Ah, there is Pen. We must go now.'

Everything seemed to churn inside Mia. Could she do it? she asked herself. Should she do it? What would Gideon think of her? Would he despise her—or would he take her in his arms and hold her close? She wished she knew. She did not think she would ever have the courage necessary.

Yet that night after dinner as Gideon and

Madame le Bret sat before the chess board, Mia did quietly slip away.

It was a strange night—great clouds massed in the sky, but every now and then the moon moved from behind one and the lagoon and mountains were bright again. Mia had chosen to wear a green dress—and then had hesitated, nearly tearing it off, for if Gideon truly loved her, she need not wear the colour he had once admired. It should make no difference. Yet she wanted to look good in his eyes.

She found a rock near the lagoon and sat staring at one of the biggest palm trees she had ever seen. The seed had obviously fallen into a pocket in the rocks and the tiny plant had grown, becoming sturdier each year until now the huge palm tree seemed to be growing out of rocks.

Was that how love grew, she wondered—slowly, bravely, despite discouragement?

She could still remember the first time she had seen Gideon, standing among the guests waiting to be greeted by their hosts, Ian's parents. He had stood out, head and shoulders above the others, yet had it been that that had attracted her attention? Or was it the way his eyes had gazed at her, compellingly magnetic?

Later he had apologised for his rudeness in staring at her, using as an excuse the fact that she reminded him of someone, Mia remembered. But was *that* the truth? Never once since he had known that she was Annys's daughter had he remarked on the resemblance between them. Nor was there any. Had he, then, as Madame le Bret was sure, fallen in love with her at the beginning?

She fidgeted on the hard rock. It seemed impossible. Never once had he given any sign of loving her, Mia thought. It must be wishful thinking on Madame le Bret's part. Was she wise to take the old lady's word and risk a sarcastic snub from Gideon? How could she tell him bluntly that she loved him?

Mia decided not to make a plan or try to make use of Gideon's Achilles heel, as Madame le Bret called it. Mia would not hide, nor play on Gideon's compassion. She would say straight out: 'I am not in love with Toby and I never was. I used it as an excuse because I thought you loved Annys and so I had to get away.'

Surely, she asked herself, that would tell Gideon all he needed to know?

A cloud passed over the moon. A tattered fragile cloud so that the moonlight could still drift through in stray fingers over the sky. She shivered as if it was suddenly cold.

And a child cried.

Mia stiffened. There were no children near. The small village where Madame le Bret's staff lived was a good two or three hundred yards away from the house, so a child's cry could not be heard from the beach.

The child cried again, a pitiful, frightened

263

wail. Mia stood up, turning round to try to see from which direction the cry came. She told herself it must be an animal . . . some strange tropical animal whose cry was like a child. Perhaps a monkey? There were quite a number in the forest, though few came down as close to the house as this. Yet was it a monkey's cry?

The cry came again. Mia walked across the sand in the direction of the sound. The way led through a group of young trees, a part she had never been to before. Now the moon sailed in the sky, unfettered by clouds, and everything was vividly bright. Mia found a track through the trees and as she walked the cry grew louder. It was quite definitely that of a child . . . !

The path stopped before a huge triangular rock that seemed to be balanced on a pinpoint yet was, as she touched it, solid. There were strange carvings on the rock and she wondered if at some time it had been one of the islanders' gods.

Ahead of her was flat ground with a few stunted bushes half hidden by the white mist that floated low above their bare branches. A strange eerie mist that had a fragrance she could not describe. A cloying smell that was attractive and yet, somehow, frightening.

She began to walk forward and stopped as her foot sank into the squelchy mud. . . It must be a marsh!

She heard a shout—and turned while still moving, not seeing the small rock before her, falling flat on her face into the muddy swamp. Feeling the sucking clawing fingers of the mud as it closed over her face and hands.

She lifted her head and screamed as she tried to stand up, her feet sinking deep into the mud.

'Don't fight it—I'm coming!' Gideon shouted just as the moon vanished from sight and the dark made it all even more frightening—but almost immediately she felt his strong hands lifting her, steadying her as her feet found the firm ground, brushing her dress, wiping her face with his handkerchief.

'I was—scared,' she gasped, still breathless, as he tried to wipe her face. The moon chose that moment to appear and she saw laughter in his eyes as he stared down at her.

Stiffly she tried to move out of his arms.

'I'm glad you find it amusing,' she snapped.

'My poor Mia,' he said, and the laughter was gone. 'I wish you could see yourself. It wasn't funny at all—it could have been very serious, but . . .'

Mia looked down at her pretty frock that was smeared with the dark evil-smelling mud. She shivered. 'It smells!'

'It'll all wash off,' he said comfortingly, 'but what on earth were you doing round here? That's why the rock is there, as a warning to the swamp.'

Mia stood very still, listening, not to Gideon, but for the child's cry. She was very conscious that his arm was still round her, but there was only silence. The child—if it had been indeed a child—had stopped crying.

'What were you doing here?' Gideon repeated, shaking her gently.

Mia looked up at him with frightened troubled eyes. 'It was like a nightmare,' she said slowly. 'It all began with the trap—and then I heard—heard the child crying. You won't believe me, I know—you'll say I'm lying.' Her voice rose a little. 'I'm always lying to you. I don't know why. I've never lied so much before to anyone. But I'm sure it was a child crying.'

'I was on the beach when I heard it. It came from this way—over there, the other side of the marsh, only I wasn't sure how far the marsh stretched and—and the child sounded frightened and I had to find it . . .'

She looked up at him earnestly. 'You do see that, don't you, Gideon? I had to find the child. It sounded so frightened . . .' Suddenly she began to shiver and his arms held her close. 'You don't believe me, do you, Gideon— you don't believe I heard a child crying, do you? You think I did this on purpose to—' She stopped abruptly, for the tears were perilously near.

'I do believe you heard a child crying,' he said.

She was so startled that the tears stopped of their own accord as she leaned back to look at his face.

'You see, Mia, there is a small boy who's always running away—at least, his parents say he is, but I believe he walks in his sleep, wakes up miles away and is terrified. I'm trying to persuade them to have medical treatment for the child. His name is Emile and I'm afraid one day he may get into real trouble.'

'Then—then—' she paused. 'Why has he stopped crying?'

'Perhaps he's tired. I'll shout.' Gideon took his arms away from her shoulders and cupped his hands to his mouth. He called: 'Emile—Emile—we've found you!' several times in French.

It was after the third call that the child cried again, a shrill frightened call.

'Stay here,' Gideon said to Mia. 'I'll edge my way round.'

'Please let me come with you,' Mia gasped, looking at the white mist that floated low over the hidden danger.

He smiled, 'All right, but hold my hand. I'm afraid your dress is a write-off.'

She looked down at the torn chiffon rags. 'It doesn't matter.'

They edged their way round the narrow path of hard earth, Gideon's warm hard fingers holding her hand so tightly that she was afraid of nothing, only conscious of the need to reach the child before he panicked and fell into the marsh.

They found the little boy in a hollow; he must have tripped over a tree root and fallen face down, his arms stretched, his clutching hands outspread, his fingers sinking into the marsh. Fortunately he had not moved, nor was his face near the swamp. He was crying bitterly, but when Gideon lifted him up and carried him, talking to him gently, the child's sobs died down.

'We can cut through up here to the road. How d'you feel about waiting here for me while I carry him home?' Gideon asked, looking down at Mia.

'I'd—I'd rather walk with you,' Mia said with a shudder.

The moon had gone again behind a cloud, but occasionally brief glimpses of light showed them the road as they approached the groups of thatched huts.

Gideon shouted and two men came running. There was an outcry of French and then several women came, one wailing that she had not missed the boy—that he deserved a thrashing.

Mia was glad her knowledge of French enabled her to understand what was being said—though it was a strange kind of French, as she heard Gideon being stern, saying the child had walked in his sleep, that one day the child would die and it would be his parents' fault. That tomorrow, the child must be taken to the doctor.

'It can be cured and then your son will never roam.' Gideon finished.

Mia was aware that everyone was staring at her as she stood slightly behind Gideon, and she knew how terrible she must look, covered with black evil-smelling mud. But she didn't care.

They walked down the road to the house.

'How are the feet?' Gideon asked once.

'Fine,' she said, and knew that once again she had lied to him. 'Actually, they're awful,' she confessed. 'Maybe it's the high heels.'

She was startled when Gideon turned and lifted her off the ground, walking as easily as if he held a feather in his arms.

'I—I can manage . . .' she began.

She could see his smile as the moon came from behind a cloud. 'So can I.' They were silent for a moment before Gideon spoke again. 'Tell me, Mia,' he said casually, 'what did you mean when I found you and you said it began as a trap? A trap for whom? For me?'

She looked up at him. His face was very close to hers as he smiled down at her. 'Go on,' he said. 'I won't eat you.'

She was glad the mud had stained her cheeks so that he could not see her blush. 'It—I—somehow—' she began.

He smiled. 'Suppose I start it for you? My beloved grandmother planned the trap—

269

right?'

Mia swallowed. 'Right,' she said weakly.

'I thought so. It's the first time in years she's asked me to play chess with her, then you vanished and I saw my dear naughty grandmother keep looking at the clock when she thought I wasn't watching, so when she said she was worried about you, I knew something was up.'

'You're so clever,' said Mia. It was weak, but the first thing she could think of to say while she tried to remember what she had planned to tell him.

He chuckled. 'I have to be when two brilliant women plan against me. Now, was her plan that you should get into trouble—lost, perhaps? Then I would rescue you while you fainted gracefully in my arms? It sounds so like my dear Gran!' He chuckled again.

Mia swallowed. 'It was—in a way. You see, there is something she said I had to tell you and—and I couldn't.'

He stopped dead, staring down at her. 'Why not?'

'I . . .' Mia took a deep breath. 'Look, Gideon, this is the real truth. Madame le Bret did suggest the plan, but I—I couldn't go through with it. I sat down by the lagoon so that you could see me at once. I was going to tell you, then. . . then I heard the child crying and—'

'You forgot me?' Gideon began to walk

270

again, still carrying Mia easily. 'Wouldn't it have been more sensible to call me and then we could have searched for the child together?'

'He didn't cry all the time. He kept stopping. I was afraid he'd stop and I wouldn't know where the cry had come from.'

They had reached the garden now. Gideon pushed open the low wicket gate and walked on to the lawn.

'So we found the child, and now here I am and you can tell me what it is that Grand'mère, bless her, says you should tell me.'

'I think—I think I'd tell you more easily if I was standing up,' said Mia.

The moon was bright now and she saw his face stiffen. 'In other words you'd rather not be in my arms,' he said coldly.

Suddenly Mia understood what the old lady had meant about unintentionally hurting people. 'I don't mean that, Gideon. I like it—I mean . . .' Her cheeks burned.

He steadied her as he stood her up on her feet. 'Make up your mind,' he said, his voice still cold. 'One moment you say it's easier to talk when out of my arms, the next moment you say you like being in them.'

Mia caught hold of his arm desperately. 'Please, Gideon, let's stop hurting one another. I didn't mean it that way. It's just that—that when I'm in your arms I can't . . . can't talk or think properly.'

'What did you say?' Gideon asked, his voice very quiet.

Mia swallowed. 'Just that—just that—Oh, Gideon, I don't want to go to Mahé—I'm not in love with Toby and I never was, but I thought you were in love with—with Annys and I—I had to get away as I thought you — you mightn't want to marry Annys if you knew she had—had me, and . . .' The words tumbled out of her mouth, not making sense to her, yet having to be said.

'I only lied about everything because I wanted you and Annys to be happy,' she struggled on. 'I've always loved you, but . . .'

Gideon's hands clamped down on her shoulders painfully. 'Mia,' he said sternly, 'repeat the last sentence.'

Suddenly she was laughing and the tears were not far. 'I've always loved you, Gideon, from the first time I . . .'

He gave her no time to finish the sentence, for he caught her close to him, his mouth coming down, warm and hard, on hers. She put her arms round his neck, closed her eyes, and the world seemed to be far away.

'I've always loved you, Mia,' he said softly, and then kissed her again. It was a long time before he let her go, and then they both heard the tinkle-tinkle of Madame le Bret's little bell.

Gideon grinned. 'Impatient to hear the results! Let's tease her for a bit?' he said, as he scooped Mia up in his arms. 'What made you

272

think I loved Annys?' he asked.

'The way you look at her.'

'Have you ever seen the way I look at you?'

Mia began to laugh. 'Your grandmother told me . . .'

'She talks too much,' Gideon said, bending to kiss Mia's mouth, 'bless her. Did I ever tell you that I love you, Mia?' he asked in an affected voice.

'Only once, you miserable creature,' Mia joked back.

The bell tinkled again. 'Perhaps we should go, she might be in trouble,' she said anxiously.

Gideon lifted her off the ground and carried her towards the house. 'Only because she has no patience,' he said with a laugh.

'She said that hate and love walk hand in hand,' Mia told him, 'that you only really hate a person when you love him.'

He smiled down at her. 'Good grief, I hate to think how much I must hate you, then!' He carried her straight to where Madame le Bret was sitting in her wheelchair, her face anxious.

'Mia, my darling child!' she cried in alarm, as Gideon put Mia on the couch. 'What has he done to you? You were so long.'

Mia sat up, straightening what was left of her green frock. 'It—it took rather a long time,' she explained, her face grave as she tried not to laugh.

'But the mud—your lovely frock—' Madame le Bret cried. She turned to Gideon.

'What did you do?'

He came to kiss her. 'Little Emile was sleep-walking again. We found him near the marsh and Mia fell in.'

'Oh, is that all?' said Madame le Bret, her face suddenly clouded, her voice disappointed.

Mia could bear to tease her no longer. She went to kneel by the wheelchair, taking the frail veined hands in hers, laying them against her cheek. 'No, it isn't all, Madame le Bret,' she said softly. 'There's lots more to tell you.'

She saw the joy in the old lady's eyes. 'You mean you . . . ?' She looked up questioningly at Gideon.

He came and knelt by the other side of the chair, putting his arms round his grandmother and round Mia. 'Yes, Grand'mère, you're the first to know. You've gone and got yourself a granddaughter!'

'Oh, my darlings!' sighed Madame le Bret, and promptly burst into tears.

'That's a nice thing to do,' Gideon teased gently as she dried her eyes.

'I'm so happy, I wept for joy,' she told him. She kissed Mia. 'My darling child, tomorrow it will be your party—we will tell the world the good news.'

'No, it's your party . . .' Mia began.

Gideon took command. 'No, Mia, it's *our* party,' he said. 'We'll all share it.'

He was right. As usual, Mia thought, but— oddly enough—this time she didn't mind.

274

Chivers Large Print Direct

If you have enjoyed this Large Print book and would like to build up your own collection of Large Print books and have them delivered direct to your door, please contact **Chivers Large Print Direct**.

Chivers Large Print Direct offers you a full service:

✧ **Created to support your local library**

✧ **Delivery direct to your door**

✧ **Easy-to-read type and attractively bound**

✧ **The very best authors**

✧ **Special low prices**

For further details either call Customer Services on 01225 443400 or write to us at

Chivers Large Print Direct
FREEPOST (BA 1686/1)
Bath
BA1 3QZ